A Marker to Measure Drift

Also by Alexander Maksik

You Deserve Nothing

A Marker to
Measure Drift

Alexander Maksik

JOHN MURRAY

First published in Great Britain in 2013 by John Murray (Publishers)
An Hachette UK Company

1

© Alexander Maksik 2013

A portion of this work was previously published, in different form,
as 'The Barbarians' in *Narrative Magazine* (Winter 2011).

Grateful acknowledgment is made to Carcanet Press Limited and United Agents
LLP for permission to reprint an excerpt from 'Sick Love' by Robert Graves from
Complete Poems in One Volume (Carcanet Press) and from *Collected Poems:
1975* (Oxford University Press). Reprinted by permission of Carcanet Press
Limited, on behalf of print rights, and United Agents LLP, on behalf of electronic
rights on behalf of: The Trustees of the Robert Graves Copyright Trust.

This is a work of fiction. All incidents and dialogue, and all characters with the
exception of some well-known historical and public figures, are products of the
author's imagination and are not to be construed as real. With the exception of actual
historical events relating to the Liberian civil wars, the situations, incidents, and
dialogues concerning those persons are entirely fictional and are not intended to depict
actual events or to change the entirely fictional nature of the work. In all other
respects, any resemblance to persons living or dead is entirely coincidental.

A CIP catalogue record for this title is available from the British Library

Hardback ISBN 978-1-84854-805-3
Ebook ISBN 978-1-84854-808-4
Trade Paperback ISBN 978-1-84854-806-0

Printed and bound by Clays Ltd, St Ives plc

John Murray policy is to use papers that are natural, renewable and recyclable products
and made from wood grown in sustainable forests. The logging and manufacturing processes
are expected to conform to the environmental regulations of the country of origin.

John Murray (Publishers)
338 Euston Road
London NW1 3BH

www.johnmurray.co.uk

For the tall man alone in the
gardens of the Reggia di Colorno

The excursion is the same when you go looking for your sorrow as when you go looking for your joy.

—Eudora Welty, "The Wide Net"

Take your delight in momentariness,
Walk between dark and dark—a shining space
With the grave's narrowness, though not its peace.

—Robert Graves, "Sick Love"

I

NOW IT WAS NIGHT.

Jacqueline hadn't eaten since the flattened chocolate bar she'd found on the step outside the pharmacy.

God's will, her mother said.

The fortune of finding food when it was most needed. Just when she didn't think she could stay upright any longer, here was food.

God's will, her mother had said for the fortune of the airplane. She'd said it for the man with the truck. And the fruit pickers in Murcia. And the woman who had the brother who drove another truck. And the Senegalese girl in Alicante who helped her up when she rolled off the park bench in her sleep. Who took her home to her family, who fed her rice and chickpeas and gave her water. The grace of God, her mother had said. For the woman who found her unconscious in the sand on a beach outside of Valencia, who walked her to the sea and wiped Jacqueline's face with a dishrag that smelled of glass cleaner, who bought her coffee with milk and sugar and two sweet magdalenas. God for the Moroccan men who were arrested while Jacqueline walked undisturbed onto the ferry in Valencia. For the cove in Palma, where she found cardboard boxes and a dirty blue blanket folded on a flat stone.

On and on her fortune went.

And for the man who'd beaten her on the beach in Málaga?

For the diarrhea?

For the absence of food?

For the bearded man and his immaculate teeth?

We pay for our sins, for the sins of others, her mother said. Anyway, we can't understand.

SHE KNEW SHE COULD NOT STAY IN THAT TOWN. Not with all the people streaming off the ferries. She sat upright on a bench. She watched them eat French fries stuffed into the tops of their gyros. They stood in line at a small shop advertising the best in the world. She watched the man slicing meat from a giant turning pile, could see him painting the bread with oil and tossing it onto the grill, could see him squirt white sauce from a bottle onto the hot bread. There were tomatoes and onions. She watched him roll and wrap them with wax paper, and hand them across the counter along with cold cans of Coca-Cola. The smell of the meat and its fat, the smell of thyme and the grilling bread all blew toward her. She watched the tourists waiting in line. She watched bits of the meat falling to the ground, the sandwiches thrown away, half eaten.

What it took for her not to stand up and cross the square and dig for food.

But she was not beyond pride, so instead she ate the chocolate bar and tried to appear happy and bored. This was, she'd decided, the appropriate attitude. You must not be desperate.

She watched policemen walk past and tried to appear cheerful as she ate her candy bar. She ate as if she might throw it away at any moment, as if eating were an entertainment, as if it were something to do. She thought, Perhaps when it's dark I'll go to the trash, but she saw that the square would never go dark.

A band was setting up. The tourists kept coming. The lights came on. There were more and more police. She stood and stretched her legs. She felt as if she might lose consciousness and sat back down. She waited until the blood returned to her head, until the feeling of nausea had eased. She stood up again and left the square, turning onto one of the small streets, thinking she might find a trash bin in a darkened corner. But every street was burning with white light. The stores sold gold and T-shirts and alcohol and food. Everywhere was food. And the tourists pushed against one another and plodded along, as bored as the shopkeepers, who eyed Jacqueline as she passed. Everything was shining with light, the narrow stone streets and the white walls, and the food, the drums of ice cream under glass, and the turning meat, and the faultless rows of tall plastic water bottles, cold in the refrigerators, all of it white under the light.

There was a large foam cup of ice cream on a ledge outside the window of a jewelry store. For a moment she thought it was part of the display, a prop for the gold chains. Then she saw there was a spoon stuck into it. As if it were hers. As if she'd ordered it. She moved to the side so that the cup was in front of her, so that she put herself between the street and it. She pretended to consider the gold. She shifted Saifa's red school pack from her shoulder to her hand, hoping it might look something like the purses she'd seen the women carrying up and down these narrow alleys. It would take one movement—an open palm, a turn of the hips, a sweep of the hand—and then she'd be moving along like the rest of them, eating as she walked.

She could feel it. Cup. Spoon. The ice cream cold in her mouth. Bits of chocolate.

A man appeared in the doorway.

He took a pack of cigarettes from his breast pocket and shook one out.

He wore a clean blue shirt, collar sharp as knife points.

He lit the cigarette and looked at her. She looked back and smiled.

"Nice," she said. The word felt misshapen and dry in her mouth.

He glanced down at her feet, over at the pack, and back

to her eyes. She smiled again. She could feel her heart. "Have a nice night," she said, turned, and walked away toward the square, leaving the ice cream melting in its cup.

She followed a road lined with eucalyptus trees and then a sign with the picture of an umbrella and a sequence of rolling waves. The road was darker and darker. She was on a hill now and could see the white lights of an airport in the distance, an occasional plane gliding away from the island. She walked for miles along the dark road, following the signs to the beach.

The beach, this beach, she decided. She would go and sleep. She'd sleep and sleep and sleep.

Like the dead, her mother whispered, a little drunk, sitting at the kitchen table in the early morning, looking out across the lawn to the ocean.

———

THERE WERE LIGHTS on steel lampposts running along the beach road. At one end a mountain of rock shot upward into the dark. She walked down the hill, past closed restaurants with hand-painted signs and sandwich boards chained to trees. She descended the few steps to the sand and vanished into the shadow of the mountain, its peak invisible in the blackening sky.

She dropped the pack and removed her rubber sandals and pushed her swollen feet into the cool coarse sand. Now she heard the sea. Or now she became aware of it.

The wind moved over her skin, cooler than she'd felt since arriving on the island the night before.

She leaned against the wall and listened to the water drawing and breaking, drawing and breaking. Above the beach the first lamppost pressed a coin of light onto the concrete sidewalk. She watched those coins stretch off in a slow curve along the road in the direction of the discos.

Barefoot, she walked a few feet away toward the sea, pushed down her underwear, and squatted.

The urine burned and felt thick, as if it were turning to something solid. She needed water. She finished, waited for the last drops to fall to the sand, and shook her hips the way Saifa used to. Then she returned to her dark corner. From the pack she withdrew the blue blanket, unfolded the neat square, and lay down on the cold beach. She drew the fabric over her body and then her face and fell asleep.

That night she dreamed of the bearded man. They were holding hands, laughing together on the lawn.

———

IN THE MORNING she woke with coarse dark sand blown across her face and piled up against her back in a smooth slope. It was in her hair and in her mouth, caught between her lower lip and her gums. She gently removed the grains from her lashes and from the corners of her eyes. She rose onto her knees. The sand slid down the back of her neck and caught in the waistband of her skirt. She shook her head, flinging sand from her hair, spitting it from her mouth, running her tongue over her teeth, along her gums. Then, still kneeling, she opened her eyes.

The sun was just rising. The wind had turned and was blowing hard offshore. She'd heard laughter in the night. It had been far away, coming in across the water or drifting from the other end of the road. Now there was no one. As far as she could see there was no one anywhere. But surely the shops would open, and the cafés above the beach with their tables set beneath colored awnings. People would come. She couldn't leave anything here. She would need to be clean.

She looked out at the water. Small waves were suspended in the powerful wind, blown hollow, their peaks torn off before they fell to the sand with a crushing sound. She walked down the steep beach to the water, where she raised her skirt and slipped her feet into the foam lit white against the black sand. It stung where the glass had sliced her right heel, where the wire had cut her left ankle.

She liked the stinging because it was sharp.

The salt will prevent infection, her mother said.

She liked her feet against the rough sand and the way the water pulled the sand from beneath her feet. She watched the waves coming in again and again and again. She leaned back into the wind and waited to decide.

She did not know how to decide. She'd come to this point. That was undeniable. She was here, while before she'd been somewhere else. She'd come here by deciding. She could not remember how she'd decided. Or even the moment of decision or the consideration. But she must have. Logic insisted. Still, now she did not know how to decide. So she waited. And when the sun had been up over the low hills for a few minutes and already, this early, she could feel the heat of it, she decided to stay.

Yes. She would stop here.

Perhaps it was because of the water on her feet. Perhaps it was because she was tired.

Look, her mother said. Look at the sparkling water. Look at the color. The sun in the sky, the orange morning, all of it evidence of intervention, everything, all of it, a convergence, the will of God.

And this ugly yellow dog?

Jacqueline watched as it passed by on the road above,

clicking its nails along the sidewalk, tongue lolling out. What? He is also God?

Her mother only smiled and looked away.

Jacqueline returned to her camp. She shook the sand from the blanket and folded it in half, then into quarters. She slid the square into the thin white grocery bag and smoothed the plastic flat and gathered it together and turned it three times before tying a loose knot. She fit it into her pack. She leaned against the wall with the sun on her face and brushed the sand from her feet and slipped them into her sandals.

———

THE TIDE WAS GOING OUT, leaving behind pools of clear water and small spits of wet black sand. She climbed up onto the rocks and followed them away from the wide beach. It took only a few minutes before she could no longer see the stretch of hotels behind her.

She was looking for a place to live.

She hadn't thought about it this way when she'd pulled her skirt to her knees and walked through the water around the dark and giant outcropping. But that's what it amounted to.

There were many caves in the rock, but all too low. They'd take on water with the rising tide. But she could see they were deep, and soon she found one above the sand at the very back of a beach shaped like a long tongue with its tip pressed flush against the edge of the dark cliff. She climbed up the rocks to just below the entrance and looked down at the sand still shining wet. The mouth of the cave, only a few feet above her now, pronounced not an O, but an M. Three pale swallows rested on its bottom lip, a rounded ledge of rock.

You must be careful, her mother said. To break an ankle would be to destroy your life. Better to fall and crack your skull open and die.

Jacqueline made her way to the edge of the cave. The birds screamed and flew off to a nearby boulder, where they stood and watched her.

She swung her pack up harder than she'd meant to. It skidded across the floor and vanished into the darkness. Then she brought her body up onto the ledge. This was the only move, a step, two steps, that posed any threat. The rock was damp and not quite flat. Her right foot, which would require all of her weight, could slip out from under her, and if that happened she would fall.

Her foot held. She leaned forward onto her hands and drew herself into the cave. She turned and sat and looked out from the shadows at the sea. She was light-headed and felt for a long moment that she might lose consciousness. She slid deeper into the cool cave, so that only her feet were in the sun.

She smelled crushed ginger in a hot, dry pan.

Hours passed and it was late afternoon when she woke. She would have to eat. It was no longer possible to ignore it. She was nauseated and weak and cold. Sunlight cut deeper into the cave. She'd been sleeping on her back, but now rolled onto her stomach and turned so that she faced the sea. She rested her chin on her interlaced fingers. She watched the tide coming in, swallowing the narrow beach. The light was turning soft and for the smallest moment it reminded her of the yellow sand at Robertsport. But now there was only her body. There was nothing left for memory except for the memory of food. She might have fallen back to sleep if not for the nausea and her cramping stomach.

But you must not sleep, her mother said.

Jacqueline knew this problem.

Your mind knows you need food, but your body has aban-

doned the idea. This is when you must eat. It is your last
chance. When your mind agrees with your body, you will die.

In a park in Alicante, she'd heard stories from three Tuni-
sian women. Stories of people falling asleep in northern cities. Fall asleep in the cold and you die of cold, they said.
They told her about drunken men who pissed themselves,
their wet pants freezing to the sidewalk. In Paris or Berlin
or Prague or Amsterdam or London. Wherever it was those
women were going. They said, There you die and people step
over your body until the police come and tear you off the
sidewalk and take you away.

Jacqueline had said nothing. She listened and remembered the gray cashmere coat her mother had sent for Christmas. It lay on her bed folded in its white box. And while
the women whispered their warnings Jacqueline could feel
the soft wool in her fingers, could see herself, collar up
against the vicious wind, as she crossed Blackfriars Bridge.
She could remember no one on the sidewalks.

She left the pack in the dark and made her way, taking
tentative steps, out of the cave and down. It was difficult to
balance. There was so much noise. The wind and the small
waves crashing and the rising tide. There was all the light
reflecting off the sand and the water.

As she moved through tide pools and across the worn
rocks, she forgot where she was walking, and then where
she was on the earth. She remembered that she'd made a
decision to stay in this place but could not say what this
place was, so she reminded herself that if she were to fall she
might split her head open, or drown, or break an ankle and
that she'd have to be cautious wherever she was, that she did
not want to die yet, after all the opportunities she'd had to
die, she would not die here of all places. Then she felt her
feet touch the coarse sand of the black beach where she'd
spent the first night. She sat down with her back to the rocks
and again watched the sidewalk curve away from her.

THE BEACH WAS FULL of glistening people spread out on towels and on chairs beneath umbrellas and there was the smell of meat being cooked and everywhere, it seemed, everywhere there was something to eat.

She walked down to the edge of the sea and splashed water on her face and over the back of her neck. She drew herself up and turned and walked with as much confidence as she could muster. At the seawall, she climbed the stairs and went to a bench, where she sat and adjusted her expression and set herself to appear purposeful and at peace. She crossed her right knee over her left and when the skirt drew up to reveal her legs, she left the skin exposed. She raised her chin and extended her arms out across the back of the bench, a posture, it seemed to her, of ease and openness. As if she might be thinking about the beauty of that strange dark blue sea, or waiting for a lover, or for her children and her husband.

Now the sun was low and the wind had come up. The sunbathers returned their sunscreen and magazines and books to their bags. They pulled on their shirts and dresses and hats. A thin girl leaned over so that her long light hair hung free. She sprayed it with something from a bottle and then pulled a brush through over and over. Between the brushstrokes, the sunlight came and went, came and went.

Jacqueline waited, leaning back, with her arms still spread out behind her—a young woman come to sit and watch the sunset. Two policemen walked along the sidewalk. She felt sick again and concentrated on the mast of a sailboat gliding around the point from the direction of her cave.

They didn't stop and when she saw their backs, and

could no longer hear them speaking, she returned her foot to the ground and leaned forward with her elbows on her knees, chin in her hands.

The beach was emptying and she was strong enough to stand and return to the sand, but now there were sturdy, handsome men coming out to stack the chairs and clear the trash. They took their time as the sun continued to fall, stopping to talk to one another, scooping up half-empty bottles of water. They collected grease-stained paper bags and soda cans, both of which appeared heavy in their hands. Nothing looked empty to her and the slowness of the men made her angry. She could not wait any longer. She stood up too fast and steadied herself on the railing. When the world came back to center, she prepared to walk.

It would be a stroll along the shoreline. She would be reflective. A thin woman recovering her life.

She descended the steps and walked onto the black sand, which was still very warm. All along the beach, the men were stacking the plastic chairs. She went to the edge of the sea and walked with her feet in the water. The trash bags were in piles. There was a woman and a man, an older boy chasing two young girls running figure eights in the shallow water. Jacqueline stopped and looked at the sea. There were more boats now. Sunset cruises. Music rose and fell, warped by the wind.

She did not look at the family.

Please leave.

Please go.

Please leave something. Please leave something, she thought. What she meant was, please leave *me* something, but she would not say it, not even to herself. She set her eyes on a sleek speedboat tearing across the horizon, its bow rising and then falling to slap the surface of the water.

Please.

Prayer, her mother said.

She turned and they were gone and Jacqueline saw that they'd left something.

Answered.

She would not race to anything. Or from it. That was more important. She would be slow in all things.

She sat in their depressions. Then, as if it had been hers all along, she reached over and took the bottle and unscrewed the top and turned it to her lips and drank. The water was warm and as it filled her mouth and ran down her throat, she began to cry. She felt something solid pass across her tongue, a piece of bread maybe, or a bit of onion.

It was so often relief that made her cry. Not pain or disappointment or horror or terror, but instead it was relief from those things. Relief and, sometimes still, love. She drank it all, nearly half a liter. She knew to drink bit by bit, but did not, so the water hurt her throat and then there was a twist of pain in her stomach, and then that sick hollowness at the top of her chest.

Patience, her mother said. And faith.

Jacqueline reached for the bag and laid it on the sand between her feet and tore it open. Inside was crumpled foil lined with white wax paper and when she'd spread it all out, she found a piece of flatbread the size of her palm and there were also scraps of roasted lamb. They'd been salted and rubbed with thyme leaves and in brighter light they'd have shone. She counted the pieces of meat. Seven of them the size of her fingertips and an eighth piece as long and thick as her little toe, which was there on the sand for comparison. She touched the bread and found the side on which the sauce had been spread. She tore it in half and collected the meat from the paper and made a sandwich, and then she ate with as much control as she could find in herself. She chewed the first bite and counted her jaw closing twenty times before she swallowed.

To be elegant, to be graceful, to be beautiful, we must do everything slowly. Nearly everything. There are some things that require us to be quick. But those things are powerful only because we do everything else slowly. One thing makes the other. Count if you're not sure.

Jacqueline counted and looked at her mother, but it was not the counting that put her on the sand, made that narrow face, those soft black eyes appear before her, made her speak, made her raise her chin, made her laugh, it was not the counting. It was the thyme.

Thyme was in her jollof. Heavy in it. Heavier than anyone's. It did not disappear behind the tomato paste, beneath the ginger. Less salt, more thyme. You roast it dry in an iron pan first with the black pepper and the chili seeds and salt. Roast it dry just until it begins to smoke and then add the oil and the onions. Then you start the rest. You do everything slowly, her mother said.

Cooking, the only domestic work her mother allowed herself.

Jacqueline's stomach twisted and cramped. Still, the pleasure. She hated the stale and acrid taste of her own mouth. It was the taste of hunger and now it had been replaced by flavors of fat and salt, bread and thyme. It was not enough, but now she had eaten, she had had some water. Now she could get control of herself. Now she could see what was there.

There was nothing to see in the sun or the water. Maybe there was something in the boats, she thought. Maybe there was something there. She liked boats, though she knew nothing about them and had traveled on only a few in her life and most of those, recently. She found them exotic and mysterious in their simplicity. It was that a boat rested on the surface of the water. That was all. Just that it did that. It was not the traveling or the adventure or the freedom. She was not interested in sailors or fishermen. Just the objects and the way they floated. She watched a small yacht pass across the wide bay. Then she turned away.

There were people crowding the sidewalk. There was

music playing. The sound traveled across the sand and through the wind. Jacqueline stood up. All along the beach were stacks of chairs. The men were gone. She put the empty bottle in the plastic bag, which she held by the handles, and she carried it along the beach as if it were her shopping. She dropped the foil and paper into the bin at the bottom of a set of concrete stairs and when she came to the top she began to walk, swinging the bag like it held a new dress wrapped in tissue paper.

She went to the far end where there were hotels and nightclubs and swimming pools. Across the street, lining the wide sidewalk, were tables beneath awnings. The people cheerful and attractive, washed and tanned. It was just after sunset now and the restaurants were mostly full.

There were men standing outside holding menus and slapping them against their palms, smiling at the passing tourists, encouraging them to come and eat and drink. A tall man, handsome in a loose white shirt, sleeves rolled to the elbows, with his hands clasped behind his back, bowed slightly to Jacqueline.

"Hello," he said to her.

She met his eyes. "Hello."

"Please, you come have a drink."

"No." She shook her head. "Another time."

For a moment, she wanted to ask for his help. Something in his face had stopped her. No, it was only that he'd spoken to her. Met her eyes. She would ask nothing of him. She smiled and then looked toward the end of the road and the gates of a large hotel.

"Have a drink," he said. "Dinner. Not expensive. Cheap." He nodded to a large chalkboard menu propped against a planter.

She knew better than to look at menus. "Another time," she said and walked on.

She would have to eat again. She needed more water. She could feel it coming on, the lightness, the trembling. At the end of the sidewalk, across from the hotel, there were three thin African men standing in front of a blanket spread out over the concrete. She hadn't seen Africans since leaving Spain and now she did not know what to be. It was good they were there. It meant less danger than she'd imagined. It meant permission. It meant tolerance. It meant possibility. But what should she be to them?

One of the men was squatting barefoot with his toes on the edge of the blanket, his hands clasped between his knees, while the other two stood quiet and stolid. They all three watched her come. Jacqueline stopped in front of their blanket. "Hello," she said. The man who'd been squatting stood. None of them spoke, so she looked down at the rows and rows of sunglasses. There was a stack of DVDs in plastic sleeves and animals carved out of wood—zebras and giraffes and elephants.

Not knowing why exactly, she knelt and picked up a pair of black sunglasses. She looked up at one of the men. "How much for these?"

"Ten," the one who'd been squatting said.

She nodded, picked up a wooden elephant, and turned it over. There was a small gold sticker on its back left foot.

"You want to buy?" the man said.

She shook her head and stood up. "No."

All three of the men were watching her. For a moment she thought she might fall. There were points of black spreading across the air. She had to close her eyes tight and reopen them to see clearly.

"*Tu viens d'ou?*" one of the other men asked.

She should not understand French. Not with these men.

"What?" she said.

"Where you come from?"

"The United States," she told him.

The man smiled. "You stay here?" he said and raised his chin at the hotel across the street.

"No," Jacqueline said.

"Where then?"

The others, who'd been distracted by a group of chattering American women in bikinis standing in front of the hotel gates, now turned their attention to her.

She looked toward the other end of the beach, at the massive outcropping of black rock. Beyond was her cave, the low sun filling it now with light.

"I'm not staying on this side. And you? Where are you three staying?" Jacqueline looked the tall one in the eyes.

"The other side?" He smiled again and, ignoring her question, said, "What other side?"

"In another town," she said, drawing herself up as straight as she could stand. She was angry now and was happy to feel it. "Have a good evening. Good luck with your giraffes," she said and met his eyes again, this time with a slight grin of her own, and then turned away. She began to walk and the man called out to her, "Where you stay, madame? Where you stay? In the big hotel in another town?" The men all laughed and she kept walking.

That weary arrogance. That chill grin.

Her anger kept her standing, kept food from her mind. Her mind. A thing she'd come to despise as much as the damp dust taste of her own mouth.

———

TWO EVENINGS LATER, two evenings since she'd last found food, light-headed and dizzy, she saw the tall man in front of his restaurant. He stood with a stack of menus in his hand. He was calm the way people are when they've eaten, when they've bathed, when the night is beginning. For a moment, she could smell the wet earth, see the waving palms from the porch, feel the cool air on her clean neck, hear the thrumming rain.

I must eat. She felt again a slight fissure, a rise of desperation.

"Hello."

She was more than twenty feet away, but the man spoke with an enthusiasm and volume that embarrassed her.

"Hello," he said again, accent on the second syllable, as if he'd been waiting for her all day. "You are returning."

Jacqueline smiled with a closed mouth and nodded. "I am returning."

"I'm happy for that. Thank you for returning."

She laughed at this and then, as if the energy she'd used to open her mouth and bring the sound out into the day had been her last, she stumbled. Had it not been for one of the lampposts, she'd have fallen. Before she could see again, the man had crossed the space between them, bent slightly at the waist, and inclined his head toward hers—a gesture of intimacy that, if she'd been fully aware of it, would have moved her. Still he hadn't touched her. He extended his hand as if inviting her to dance, and in a low voice, he said several times before she could see, or make sounds into words, "You are fine? Lady? You are fine?"

It had been only a few seconds, but she did not know how long she'd been hanging on the pole, how long the spreading white had been white, or even if she'd fallen to the ground and pulled herself up. Her first concern was being conspicuous and she was grateful for the man's manner.

"You will come? Please." Now he extended his right arm so that his fingers pointed in the direction of the empty restaurant and beyond to the bay.

She could not stay clinging to the metal post like a drunk. It would be better to go with the man. This was a decision. Between two things, this was the better thing. She could not risk the attention. "I'll come," she said and took the man's arm, which was warm and solid in her hand. The feeling of his skin against her palm brought a jolt of pleasure, which left her even weaker. As if now, with that arm—and it seemed then that it was not connected to any person, just a warm thing to hold, to pull her along—she could give in, leave it all up to someone, to something else. The making of decisions, the relentless arguing with herself, with her mind.

She had felt this way in Spain, sitting across from that woman in the café eating the magdalenas. Take care of me, please. Take care of me. But it lasted only until she'd finished her coffee. Eaten. It was not enough food. But it was enough food to drive away her awful mewling, her pathetic need, enough to stand up and say *gracias, gracias,* and walk out of there as if she had a place to be. A place in mind. But that was on a Spanish beach and she had been younger by months. She did not know how many.

From the moment she'd landed in Málaga, she hadn't bothered to count time. She'd realized as she stood up from her seat and begun to walk up the clean blue aisle, it was the end of luxury. The end of Bernard's cheap benevolence, the end of the cool cabin and its thin, dry air, the carts of water and food, the sharp-edged magazines, the solicitous flight attendants, *messieurs, mesdames.*

Since then, she hadn't bothered, hadn't considered it— the whole thing artificial and unnecessary. Get somewhere and live there. So what difference did it make? But she could not avoid it. Time was measured. Memory was present and there was a chronology. She knew where she was in that chronology, where she'd been: what came before Spain, what came there, and what came after. She could break it up again and again, make it smaller and smaller. All the increments of a life. She wanted to guard it all. It was just that counting time was no longer of use.

The man was guiding her to the restaurant. She wanted to say, Too much sun today. I'm dehydrated. I always forget to drink enough water. Somewhere in her stale mouth, she was turning the words into a sentence, but she could not speak.

She held on to the man's arm as he took her into the restaurant and lowered her gently into a chair. There was a hand at her back and then a cool glass before her. She drank and he, standing at her side, that warm arm drawn behind his back, the plastic bottle in his right hand, refilled the glass.

She was a customer in a restaurant. Gracious waiter. Sunset on an island. People walking along the beachfront. Holiday. What would they know, these passersby? This and the third glass of water and the man at her side brought her calm.

Now she leaned back in her chair. "I can't pay you," she said. "I don't have money with me."

"You are okay?"

"Yes, fine, thank you for the water. I should get back now."

He'd come around the table and was leaning forward, his clean hands flat on the paper tablecloth. "Stay," he said and smiled. "Stay. A little while, yes? Wait." He raised his left hand and showed her his palm. "Stay? Yes?" He smiled and left her there.

She picked up a silver knife and then returned it to the table. Hanging from the back of one of the wood and wicker chairs was her plastic bag, and in it the empty water bottle. She looked away, and out at the sky. She should leave here, gather herself up and get back before it turned any darker, but she was tired and weak, the chair was solid beneath her, and she could not make herself move. Just a few minutes longer and then she'd go. She wanted to cross her arms on the table, lower her head, and rest, but if she were to stay she must do so upright. Stand and leave. Stand and leave. But she could not. The chair was a bed. She closed her eyes.

The arm passed in front of her. Then there was a plate. A large tomato, a green pepper. Both had been stuffed and baked, the caps leaning against their respective fruit.

"Yemista," the man said and poured olive oil from a glass bottle in a green stream three hundred degrees of a circle around the plate. "Pepper and tomato. Made with rice. Eat, please."

Jacqueline looked down. There was the smell of garlic and mint.

The man had come around to the other side of the table, brought the chair out, and sat sideways, as if he wouldn't stay long.

"Please," he said again.

She shook her head. "I have no money. With me. I have no money on me now." Vapor rose from the food. It was very close to her, the smell made her dizzier. Such desire was beyond her experience.

This is God, her mother said. Take what He gives you. Don't be stubborn, young woman. Eat.

"You do not need to pay me," the man said, but when Jacqueline glanced up, her eyes rising from the food to meet his, he said, "You pay me the next day. The time after, yes? Now you're eating, yes?"

God, her mother said. All of this, God.

"Yes. Not the next day, but I'll pay you. Not tomorrow, soon."

"Not important," the man said.

She spread the paper napkin across her lap and raised the heavy silverware from the table. She drove the tines in, drew the dull, serrated blade through the baked crust of rice, the skin, the soft flesh of the tomato. She ate. Then there was nothing else—not her mother, not before Spain, not Spain, not the cave, not the Senegalese men, not this man. For those minutes there was only the food.

THE MAN HAD LEFT her alone to eat. Still, when he could, he stopped by the table, smiled at her while serving other tables, and when she'd finished, came to offer her more. She could have eaten endlessly. But after she'd sopped up the olive oil on her plate with a thick piece of bread, after she'd finished the bottle of Coke he'd placed before her next to a fresh glass, she watched him serving his customers, and then, despite every desire, stood up to leave. She did not take with her any of the bread that was left in the basket. She did not hide any of the sugar packets in her pockets. Aside from the one she'd spread across her lap, she left the paper napkins in their dented silver holder.

"You must stay," the man said. "You must have dessert. Coffee. Grappa."

"No." She had seen the frosted metal bowls of ice cream, the long-handled spoons. "No," she said. "I'm late already."

"Late?"

"I have to meet my friends," she said, her stomach already cramping.

"Yes," he looked away from her.

"I'll pay you for the food."

"No," he began and then, seeing her eyes, "Yes, yes, when you can. It is no race."

She smiled at this. Again, she wanted to know his name and nearly asked, but stopped herself by lowering her head and swallowing.

"Not race at all," he said and swept his hand back across the space between them, as if he were wiping a table clean. "You are fine for walking?"

A group of young women had arrived and were standing

at the entrance. The man glanced over his shoulder and then back to Jacqueline.

"I'm fine for walking," she said. "Thank you very much. Thank you." She felt the thickness rise in her chest and then in her throat as if she might cry. She thought of her posture, the string at the top of her head pulling her straight.

Raise your chin, young woman.

"The food was delicious."

"You are welcome," he said. "Forever you like."

"Thank you." She smiled again and now stepped away from her chair, from her good table, from her warm corner, and began to walk toward the clean young women who had taken menus from the stack on the small wooden table.

"Come," he said and pointed them to a corner of the terrace closest to the sea. "Come, beautiful ladies." Jacqueline slipped past and out onto the street as the women clicked and teetered to their table.

"Don't forget," the man said.

Jacqueline turned. The white plastic bag hung from his fingers.

"Oh." She said, "Thank you," and took it. The bag was heavy. He'd replaced the bottle.

"Thank you," she said again.

"Forever you like," the man said, smiled at her once more, and returned to his restaurant.

———

THE SUN HAD NEARLY SET and in the blue twilight stars were beginning to appear. There were shopkeepers and restaurant owners standing outside with menus beneath their arms, there were club and bar touts, and there were the tourists, mostly young like the women in the restaurant. Clean clothes. Suntanned or sunburned. She had not eaten so well since leaving. No, before leaving. How long had it been? Warm food on a plate. Flavor. She thought of the food she'd refused on the plane. She saw that tray often and now again saw the hand take it away, all the small packages unopened. If you prefer to live, the loss of appetite is a luxury. So when then? Her mind did this more and more often. It slipped away from her. She was trying to answer one question, to stay on one track, but she would lose it.

There was the bread left in the wire basket, there had been more peppers, more rice, more oil.

She had lost track of time. There were only the fundamental events of her life, the sensual elements, and the places themselves. In fact, all of it, well, no, not all (but that, she sometimes thought, was a question of time and of control), had blurred, was fading from clear image to murky sensation. Everything behind her, even the very most recent life, seemed to have lost its form or structure in her memory so that those events, those people, those places, had become clouded and obscure and existed only as a kind of aftertaste.

Saifa's room, for example, was no longer something she saw. Instead it was a feeling, a brief wash of sensation, the way a smell, burning butter, say, recalls a man whose name you remember, but whose face is impossible to recover. You cannot describe him and yet you remember him nonetheless. This blurring spread across her memory but avoided certain scenes, certain faces, the way a woman chooses one man and not another.

Her mind spun on like this. She had walked nearly to the end, where the road turned away from the sea. She stopped on the sidewalk, leaned over the railing, and looked down at the black sand, following it with her eyes to the rocks, where she could see a skirt of white foam.

She tried to answer the question.

She remembered the porch in the sense that to remember is not always something that happens to a person. To remember is an active verb also, her father had told her. More than most things, places were easier to recall with clarity. She saw their terrace. There was shade. Four chairs around a plastic table. Four green chairs around a white table. That was on one end. Then on the other, there were four chairs. These reclined and were made of metal and tan mesh. They were kept in a row, the last aligned, by its two outer feet, with the corner of the house. In the other sense of the word, she remembered lightning storms. Without any conscious provocation, the sky turned violet and was shattered by jagged veins of light. This is the show, her father said. This is the show, children, the show. He laughed high and nasal and clapped his hands. I am not your child, her mother said. I know, my love, I know, he said. But he did not know.

They drank Coca-Cola from the bottle, except for her mother, who insisted on a glass. And Saifa. When she became pregnant, she stopped drinking Coca-Cola altogether. Jacqueline did not know when this lightning storm had been, or how old she was then, or even if her sister had been born yet.

The show, the show.

She unscrewed the cap of the plastic bottle and drank. After sitting at a table, glass after glass of cold water, Coke, it was an indulgence to waste this. She capped it and returned it to the plastic bag. She was irritated with herself. Any bit of luxury and she softened, shifted, and forgot. This was the problem with fortune.

This is the problem with your God. You are lulled into faith.

Her mother in the hall mirror adjusting a pale green scarf around her neck.

Looking out at the shining black rocks, Jacqueline had been thinking she would not return to her cave, but again, she was angry for her laziness.

Nothing has changed because you've eaten this meal, her

mother said. If anything, you must be more careful. You are known. You are present in the minds of at least four people. Now you must take your plastic bag, walk across the sand, and move carefully. As always, you must do what is difficult. Despite your laziness, despite your lack of will.

Her mother sliced a lime in half lengthwise.

Jacqueline was overcome by fatigue and more than anything at that moment, she wanted to lie on the bench and close her eyes, but she walked down the steps into the dark. Her eyes felt swollen and heavy. She walked along the water to the end of the sand and climbed up onto the boulders. She moved carefully, staying low, trying to keep her hands and feet always on the rock. The tide was high and the waves broke fast and rolled up the long spits of sand spreading their white foam. It was cool and humid, the air heavy with salt. Handhold by handhold to the lip of the cave she was nearly certain was hers. At the top, she wiped her foot dry. She counted one-one-thousand, two-one-thousand, three, pushed off, and threw herself headfirst into the darkness, where she found her pack and the blanket. She spread it out across the cool, damp floor. She lay on her belly and faced the sea. There was no sound other than the breaking waves and the sloshing water.

She watched the lights traverse the bay until she gave in.

THE SOFTNESS OF THE BED began to give way to a point of pain in her belly. She shifted and the pain sharpened. She opened her eyes. The sun had just come up over the bay and was cutting into the cave. She hadn't menstruated for nearly a year, and now it had begun again. How could that be? Maybe it was the meal. But how could a single meal? She kept her eyes closed and thought of the thick pile of napkins she'd left in the restaurant. What she had kept from the ferry was nearly gone. She should have taken them. Not the sugar packets, but anyone might have taken napkins, not only a vagrant. She reached beneath herself. There was a sharp stone stabbing into her skin. She rolled it between her fingers. Only a stone. She did not open her eyes. She did not have the energy. Not for waking, not for turning her body, not for climbing, not for walking, not for finding food, not for doing what she knew she must if she insisted on living.

———————

An Algerian man selling fruit on a sidewalk in Málaga had told her a story of three women who lived with him in an illegal inland camp. They had shelter. There was water nearby, he said. They had jobs picking strawberries in a nearby greenhouse. They were paid regularly. But even so, they'd waited and held hands and stepped in front of a train. I understood, the man said. Even if I can't explain it, and don't have the courage to do it myself, I understand it. He gave her the oranges and told her that she must eat fruit if she wanted to live.

She didn't believe she deserved that quick exit, nor the romance and flash of that kind of death. Once, on a cold morning, she had been so incapable of movement that she had allowed a warm stream of urine to flow out of her while she lay on some beach wrapped in her blanket. She'd stayed lying in it, crying and shivering, as the urine turned cold. It was as close as she'd come. That was the suicide she imagined. Rot to death. Lie in the cold sand. Shit herself. Piss herself. Eat nothing. Go blank. Wait. The Algerian man had reminded her of her father, so naïve, so sure of himself. She had accepted his gift. Those oranges tasting so entirely like orange. She'd eaten while he spoke and the memory returned that flavor to her mouth. *If* you want to live, he'd said.

I will get up.

She counted down from ten as if before leaping from the rocks in Robertsport and at one she opened her eyes. A long white yacht was anchored in the bay. She could see women lying naked on the bow. The tide had retreated and below she could see the spit of black sand. Aside from the yacht and the sailboats moving far out across the horizon, she was alone. She sat up and stretched her arms above her head. Her body was sore. To stay here, she'd have to create some kind of mattress. After folding the blanket and returning it to its place, she closed the pack and slid it deeper into the cave, out of the light where it would not be seen. She moved down the rock easily. You can't prevent it, places become familiar, your body adapts. Muscle memory. She'd always liked that expression. Whatever you do, the body remembers. She slid her underwear down, brought her skirt up to her waist, and squatted behind a boulder. There was still pleasure. Still. Even this morning.

Until that was gone.

She relaxed and felt the vaguest sense of rejuvenation. To have drunk enough to piss like this. She'd left the water bottle behind. She liked the idea of saving it, keeping it away from herself. A good thing to return to. Squatting there, her feet dug into the cool sand, in the shade of the boulder, she thought of the peppers, of the rice and the thick-cut bread left in the basket.

She drew her underwear back up and stood. She needed to wash. She needed clean water. She hated the salt-stiff cotton. It burned where her skin was raw. She walked around the boulder and out to the water, letting it wash over her feet and up to her ankles. She looked out at the yacht, at the brown women on the bow deck. They were too far for her to see faces. She began to walk toward the main beach. She straightened her spine, unclenched her fists, let the weight of her hands swing her arms.

I am at leisure.

In Málaga, still carrying the remnants of her first life in her breasts and on her hips, she'd been sitting on the sand with her arms around her knees when a small blond woman with sunburned hands had shown her a peeling laminated card.

"You want massage cheap? Good strong. Yes?" The woman had demanded. "Yes?" She pointed to the rates written in neat handwriting. Five minutes, three euros. Ten minutes, five. Shoulders, feet, and back.

"No," Jacqueline had replied. "No. But thank you."

The woman took her hand and from a glass bottle poured a small green pool into Jacqueline's palm. She moved her thumbs, rubbing the oil into Jacqueline's skin, pulling the blood along.

"I have no money," she'd protested. "No money."

"Yes," the woman said. "Cheap."

Jacqueline shook her head and tried to take her hands away, but the woman held tighter.

"No money. No money." Jacqueline lowered her head and began to cry. It was as if the woman's hands were taking something from her. "No money," she said again.

She looked up and was unable to wipe her face. "No money," she said again. "I am like you. I am like you."

"Free," the woman said. "Okay? Free."

And for a few minutes she massaged Jacqueline's hands. The smell of the oil was rich and round and clean. As the woman pushed her thumbs along the muscle, Jacqueline cried and watched the small bottle in the sand, the sun through the glass, the yellow Puget label, the bright oil. When the woman released her, Jacqueline did not know how much time had passed. She raised her eyes and smiled.

"Thank you," she said. She could still feel the fingers moving against her skin.

"Thank you. I'm sorry I have no money."

"We are fine," the woman said. "We are fine, we," she'd said, taking her card out of the sand with the very tips of her thumb and forefinger, as if she were extracting a hair from a plate of food. She shook the sand off, stood up, and looked down at Jacqueline.

"Okay," the woman said.

"Okay," Jacqueline said and watched her walk down the beach, stopping at each towel, each umbrella. She fell back then, her knees pointing at the sky, and with her eyes open and the fine sand sticking to the backs of her hands, she did her best to thank God, to wish that woman well.

Now, Jacqueline walked along the black beach.

And what you're about to do? Her mother put down her book. This is not also God? This is not a plan? You still think it an accident that woman found you?

You want me to say that I am fortunate? You want me to tell you that I am blessed? Because she pitied me? That is a blessing?

How do you begin?

Excuse me, sir, excuse me, ma'am. Excuse me for bothering you.

Jacqueline walked to the waterline and followed it to the far end of the beach. The sun was strong, but not stronger than what she was used to. Still, if she were to do this, she'd need a hat. She imagined a wide white note card lying flat on a long oak desk. She wrote, *hat*. She ran her palm over her head, feeling the short hair bristle against her hand. She tied her skirt in a knot high up her thighs so that the fabric fell like drapes around her legs and she walked out into the water. The man would be there, far across the beach, up the steps. She thought of him setting his tables, filling the salt-shakers. She would need a lie. A student in New York. Columbia University like her father. And to make money, to pay for what the scholarship didn't, to make ends meet, she did this. New York is expensive. It was good enough. She had the accent when she wanted it. She knew the idioms. Her father had given her those.

The chairs had all been unchained and spread out side by side in rows, some beneath umbrellas, some in the full sun. There were families who brought their own or who sat only on towels. The local buses came and went.

There were other things, but nothing she was willing to do.

She came out of the water and began with a couple sitting on a wide red towel. The woman lay on her stomach, propped up on her elbows. The man sat at her side, stroking her back. Jacqueline preferred the people away from the chairs. The attendants made her nervous. Out here, closer to the water, she'd be less conspicuous. It occurred to her as she approached that she'd never considered whether or not she knew how to touch these strangers, but she did not turn away.

"Excuse me for bothering you," she said.

The man had watched her come, had pushed with his thumb into the woman's back in warning.

Jacqueline could see herself approaching. Thin, black woman. Bright, artificial smile.

"Excuse me," Jacqueline said again. She'd begun the sentence too far out and was afraid that with the wind, they might not have heard her. You must be polite. Above all things. "I'm sorry to bother you. Do you speak English?"

"Yes," the man said, and the woman nodded.

"I'm sorry to bother you."

Jacqueline was standing between them and the sun. The couple looked up at her. She could see herself reduced and multiplied in their sunglasses.

"Do you mind?" She said, lowering herself, careful to press her skirt between her knees, focusing on the woman, who smiled now.

"I'm sorry to bother you," she said again, kneeling on the sand. "I'm a student but I'm also a masseuse, a massage therapist, and I was wondering if you'd like—"

"Oh no no no." The man cut her off, shaking his head.

"Michael," the woman said sharply.

"No, it's fine, I certainly understand. I'm sorry to bother you both."

"Wait, please. How much for a foot massage?"

The man shook his head. "I don't mean to be rude, but as I'm sure you know, we can't buy everything we want. I'm sure *you* know this."

The woman ignored him. "How much?"

Jacqueline hadn't thought about the cost. She said, "One euro for five minutes. That's what I've been charging, but if you'd like—"

"No, that's fine. That perfectly fair," she said. "How would you like me?"

"What kind of massage do you do?" the man asked.

"Oh," Jacqueline said. "It's a combination, you know, I don't like to limit myself."

He took off his sunglasses, wiped the sweat from his nose, and looked at her.

"Swedish," she said. It was all she thought of.

The man smirked as if he knew everything about her and Jacqueline began to tremble. Not because of him, but because he'd stolen the bearded man's eyes—as dark as if they were devoid of irises. And they sparkled.

Not the glint of charm or humor or lust.

But of the other thing.

"This okay?" The woman had leaned back on her elbows. Now she was pointing her red-painted toes at Jacqueline. "It's all right," she said. "Go on. Five minutes, one euro. Ignore him." The woman laughed and rolled her eyes at the man, who shook his head and smiled at Jacqueline. He returned the sunglasses to his face. He was just a person on a beach. A holiday. There was no menace, no challenge. Jacqueline slid her skirt higher up her legs, walked her knees forward, and took the woman's small feet into her hands and rested them on her bare thighs. She took the right foot so that the heel rested between her two palms. She pushed her thumbs along the pad of the heel, along the arch, and over the ball of the foot.

"Oh, that's wonderful," the woman said, "wonderful," and let her head fall back so that her long black hair hung clear of her neck and collected behind her on the red towel.

"Look at the movie star," the man said. The woman did look like something out of a magazine—enormous black sunglasses and black bikini, head thrown back, the skin drawn tight across her throat. Jacqueline wished she had her own sunglasses. She could not tell if the man was looking at her or if he was looking out to sea. She added sunglasses to her list of things she needed to start a new life. Her thumbs moved over the feet. They were smooth as a child's.

The woman made quiet sounds of pleasure. There was the sound of the surf and of the wind rushing past.

"You have beautiful feet."

"You have great hands. My God, where did you learn to do this?"

"Oh, in New York," she said. She glanced over at the man, who was now lying on his back, his head turned away from

them, breathing as if he were asleep. "A massage school,"
she added.

She'd learned from Saifa, who had been laying her feet
in Jacqueline's lap since they were children. And it was never
the other way around. In the early morning after dancing on
the couch together, sitting on the terrace watching the dark
towering clouds come in over the ocean, Jacqueline held her
sister's feet and pressed her thumbs along the same lines,
squeezed, held Saifa's heels in her palms like warm tea-
cups, squeezed her toes and cracked the joints. And when
she'd become pregnant, idiot girl, every night talking about
the places they'd live together, all the lives they'd lead. In
Manhattan and Paris, Los Angeles, and most of all Papeete,
where their father had once been the guest of an American
businessman.

"No place in the world as pretty as Tahiti. It wouldn't be
possible. God couldn't do better. He must have made it last,"
he said. "It was the work of a master."

"Unlike this place," her mother said. "Unlike this place,
the work of an amateur, the work of a child with a crayon."

"You will go to hell for that," he said.

He kissed his wife on the forehead and she did not say
what was obvious to all of them but her father.

Imagining this woman's feet her sister's, Jacqueline had
lost track of time. Now the man seemed to be asleep. The
woman had eased down onto her back, her arms out at her
sides, palms upturned. Five minutes must have passed, but
she was not certain, so she continued, focusing on the bodies in front of her. How could they lie there like that, as if in
their own beds, the doors locked?

She no longer wanted the feet in her lap. She imagined
driving her thumbs hard into the arch. Instead she laid them
on the sand as if they were valuable.

"Over already?"

"Yes," Jacqueline said.

"Maybe I should buy another five minutes."

Without moving, the man said, "Maybe not, *dear*," saying *dear* as if it were a joke, as if he'd never use such a word to mean his wife. The woman lowered her sunglasses and rolled her eyes at Jacqueline.

As if they both shared in the joke, as if they both knew what men were like, but only Jacqueline knew what men were like.

"My dear," her father said to all three of them. "My dear, my dears." And he meant it always. He was incapable of sarcasm.

"It's a euro, please."

Jacqueline had lost her energy. She hadn't charged enough. She had no more patience for charm, for her lie, for kneeling. The man raised himself up just enough to reach back and push a hand into the pocket of a white canvas bag.

"What's that accent?" he asked with a coin in his hand. "Jamaica?"

"She speaks English perfectly. Better than you, Michael, I'm sure."

"I'm talking about her accent," he said. "Not her English."

"Just give her the money."

Jacqueline sat on her heels. She was still. She could feel everything falling from her. The weight drawing her face down, deadening her eyes.

Jacqueline put her hand out and when she felt the coin in her palm, she closed her fist and stood up. The blood drained back down into her calves, into her feet. She was no longer cut at the knees.

"So what's the accent?"

"Liberia," she said.

The woman rested her head on her long black hair, on her wide red towel, and sighed. "Thank you, thank you," she said. "Maybe we'll see you tomorrow."

"Liberia," the man repeated. He nodded as if he suddenly

knew her. "Take care of yourself," he said in a new voice, which was to mean something solemn and sympathetic.

Jacqueline nodded and walked away from them down to the water. With her back to the beach, she slipped the coin into her bra and felt it pressed solidly against the top of her breast.

She broke at the waist and washed her hands in the sea.

———

SHE BUILT A MATTRESS OUT OF GARBAGE.

The cardboard she took from a stack behind a grocery. She came out in the cold early morning when nothing moved but the stray dogs and the sea and the wind. Mostly, she took what was left. The cardboard, for example—two collapsed cases of Delica bathroom tissue. She stole a plastic bag from a city garbage can.

It's hardly stealing. It's meaningless.

In the darkness, she worked the wide metal trash bins in the alleys behind the main road. She didn't touch the food. The rotting fruit, the molding bread, the souring milk. She filled the bag with the cleanest, driest trash. She crushed it down and added more. She stole another. Wide, strong, transparent green the color of dying grass.

God sees everything. Everything.

In the early morning, when the sun lit up her cave so that not a corner was in darkness, she tore the boxes open. She spread the first on the stone floor. Each packed full, she tied the two bags together, mouth to mouth in six knots, and molded the trash to cover the length of the cardboard. The second piece went on top.

The next day while she was working, she collected the

thin plastic grocery bags that swirled around the beach like ghosts.

Later, along the perimeter of each piece of cardboard she pierced holes with a pointed stone. She rolled the plastic bags into cord, threaded the holes and bound the mattress together.

She tried a pillow of trash, but the sound kept her awake. Always crackling in her ears and in half-sleep, it spoke to her. There were voices enough, so she filled a doubled bag with sand, put it under her head, and slept without pain.

Most mornings, she woke when the cave filled with light. She dressed. She climbed down. She could have done it blindfolded.

I'd like to see you try, her mother said.

Jacqueline squatted behind the rock. She used paper only when she shit. And when she shit, she dug a hole first. As deep as her elbow.

You were nothing if not clean. Everything wrapped up neat for you, her mother said. Nothing left behind.

Her mother was changing.

Sometimes there was acid in her voice.

———

THE DARKEST MORNINGS, after the moon had gone and there was no sound on the promenade, when the only noise was blowing wind and breaking waves, she slid out of the cave and crawled down the stone.

Like a rat, her mother said.

She moved carefully around the point. There in the shadow of the great outcropping, there where she'd spent her first night, she slid her skirt from around her waist and dropped it in the sand. Her underwear too. Tank top and bra. She collected it all in her arms and stood still, and when she was sure, she moved out of the shadow and climbed the steps. She pushed the stiff silver button and the shower kicked to life. She crouched naked on her heels and washed the clothes, draping them dripping over the wall, piece by piece. Then she rose and stepped onto the metal grate. Twice, she'd done this and in those two dark mornings, naked beneath the water, beneath the soft glow of the streetlight, before the wide, empty orange street, before a skulking cat, she felt as if she were breaking open. That first instant when the water covered her, it was as if something cracked and fell from her skin, from her eyes. It was more than salt and grime. She wanted to stay longer. She always wanted to stay longer.

She collected her wet clothes and walked naked over the rocks, keeping low, careful not to slip, and eventually found her way back up the wall and into her cave. She brushed the sand from her feet and swung them inside. She laid the clothes out flat, wrapped herself in the blanket, and slept.

THE LEAST EXPENSIVE hat she could find was a white cotton visor with an adjustable Velcro band. HELLAS it said in light blue lettering. Four euros at a small market a few minutes up the road. It gave her the look of a tourist, she thought. A real souvenir.

When she began her day, she wore the visor low over her eyes. She walked the beach every morning. She was careful. She approached only the people on towels close to the water. She carried no sign, no evidence of her work. She maintained the same story, the same disposition—bright-eyed student, scratching out an island vacation before returning to school in the fall. The visor softened her, she thought. It hid her eyes, made her look earnest and enthusiastic. Like Saifa.

In the morning: HELLAS. She kept it white. Washed it in the sea. Let it bleach in the sun.

She rubbed their feet, their shoulders, their hands. Three euros one day. Two. Once, six. Some days nothing at all. She began by dragging up and down the sand from morning until sunset. But she soon saw that the only ones who called her over called after lunch, when they were groggy and at home in their pockets of sand, trusting of her—a well-spoken student, a charming accent.

Now she was an earner. Enough to buy a hat.

———

SHE CAME EVERY DAY at noon to a small gyro stand. The man was big with a scar across his forehead. He was neat, unsmiling, suspicious. But his apron was as clean as his restaurant. A counter, three stools, a takeaway window to the street. When he opened, he hung a red, white, and blue clock outside the shop. Pepsi. She marked time by the rotating soda bottles.

"Good afternoon." When she spoke to anyone she stood straight, was formal, smiled.

He nodded.

"Pork or lamb?"

"Pork today." She alternated. Pork, lamb, pork, lamb.

"French fries?"

"Of course."

"Drink?"

"Water."

He sliced the meat from the skewer and spread it on the griddle. She loved the way he snatched the hot bread from the grill, pulling it into the air, turning toward her as it crossed the space from hot station to cold and landed in front of them on a plastic cutting board beneath the counter. He went left to right, spread the sauce, the lettuce, the tomatoes.

"Onions?"

"Please."

He slid the bread onto wax paper and carried it back to the grill, where he added the meat and rolled. He turned the paper into a cone and filled the opening with French fries.

She ate at the counter. Every day at the same time. Pork, lamb, pork, lamb. They didn't speak otherwise. The man stood at the window watching the street, waiting for customers who came, stood outside, and took their food to go. No one ate at the counter but Jacqueline.

When she was finished she placed her coins on the countertop.

"Okay?"

"Best in the world."

The man would smile. Satisfied, proud, but not surprised.

She could have bought chocolate bars for less. Bags of chips. But what else did she have to spend her money on?

In this way, she was rich.

SIX NIGHTS, she's been here.

This morning she is shaken awake by a brutal dream she

can't remember. The sky is purple, paling in the east, a few stars still hanging on before the sunlight washes them away. She is struck by a terrible loneliness. It comes in the form of heavy exhaustion, of a sadness so deep she can feel it in her spine. She is debilitated. She goes out only to squat behind the rock. She does not put on her visor. She does not go to the beach. She stays at the back of the cave. She turns the mattress on its side to block the sun. One of her knots has come undone. She does not retie it.

Now there is time to think of things other than survival. It is the curse of luxury.

She has food and water and shelter. She has lined one side of the cave with flat stones to serve as shelves. Pedestals. The tube of Fresh Mint ChapStick she found in the sand stands upright like a bullet next to her toothbrush. There's a neat stack of paper napkins she keeps beneath a small smooth rock. Her sandals side by side on their own stone. There's a paper cup into which she deposits the money she brings home. Today it holds a single coin. She should go out, but she has no appetite. Hunger is no longer the burden. It is time. It is the new absence of need. The instinct is to protect yourself. To build and organize, to form your days, to apply patterns and repeat them. And she has done all of this without intention. She has built a home without meaning to. And now she wants to know what happens next.

She does not have the capacity to kill herself.

Let's be honest, her mother says. You haven't the courage for that kind of thing. No matter what you feel. It's not in you, my love.

She believes her mother is right.

And she does not have the capacity to live the rest of her life in a cave caressing the dirty feet of tourists.

Yes, but what then? There is no answer. What answer could there be? There is no one left. Even Ghankay has gone, which seems impossible. Even in her cave, so far away, it seems impossible.

London, her mother offers. Helen.

But Jacqueline ignores her. She bites into her bottom lip.

"Why doesn't he say *I*," she'd asked her father. "Why does he say President Taylor when he means *I*?"

They were watching him on television.

"Some people believe," President Taylor was saying, "that President Taylor is the problem."

Her father reached over and patted her knee. When the speech was over, she asked the same question again. It was not without accusation, not without anger. Later, she listened to the BBC as the UN unsealed Taylor's indictment: murder, torture, rape, sexual slavery, terrorism, looting, the unlawful recruitment of child soldiers under the age of fifteen, the murder and kidnapping of UN peacekeepers in the performance of their duties.

Her father looked at her and smiled a cold smile, a smile that meant, What I'm about to say is the last we'll speak of it, what I'm about to say is the final word. He said, "That's Ghankay. Exceptional men have exceptional habits, Jacqueline."

She would have pressed it, but her mother looked at her and she shut up.

"This is what happens when, all your life, you live on a hill looking down on the poor," Bernard had said, an arm around her shoulder. They were sitting side by side in the back of the Land Cruiser, sixty kilometers from the border of Sierra Leone.

He didn't know.

She'd come alone. Walked from the house. Through the streets without seeing the present world, without hearing it. Her mind was full of sound. On the way no one bothered her. The streets empty. At the hotel they nearly didn't let her in. Even her, but she looked up and the guards sighed. She passed through the gate. The pool terrace was jammed with journalists sitting on packed bags. It looked like Victoria Station during a strike. Tired-looking white people with their heads in their hands.

She'd found Bernard sitting on the floor of his room, the door open, feet on his pack. When he looked up, it wasn't with the right expression.

Now in the Land Cruiser, safely away from Monrovia, he spoke.

"Your parents are safe? Saifa?"

She nodded. He would have left without her.

"What'll you do for money?"

"Bank of America," she said. "I told you."

But there was no account and no one was safe.

She fell asleep. When she woke there was a group of LURD soldiers surrounding the truck. Boys. The one in a white NFL ON FOX T-shirt kept the barrel of his rifle pressed against her head.

She was frightened, but still she thought, Pull it.

"Answer them," Bernard said. The driver and another man, both of them as white as Bernard, looked straight ahead.

"She's sick," Bernard said.

"Firm your jaw," the boy said and with the barrel poked him hard in the temple.

There was an older one speaking to her, but she could not see him.

Where was she going?

"New York," she said, looking at the back of the driver's head.

"Why you go New York?"

"I live there."

"Passport."

"They stole it," she said. "They stole everything."

"Who do?"

"Taylor," she said. "Taylor's soldiers."

"Journalist?"

She nodded.

"Out."

The door opened and she stumbled onto the red dirt road. She hadn't noticed before, but now she could feel the camera Bernard must have hung around her neck.

The man who'd been speaking stood in front of her. He was so close she could barely see him. His skin shone and he smelled of cologne. Reeked of it. It seemed the whole road smelled the same.

"You tell that we will take action," he said. "You tell we have enough to take city. *Enough.* You tell we come dress Taylor like a woman." He stepped back. "You tell that."

She nodded. He let her back in the car. Held the door for her. Helped her in. In white letters across the back of his T-shirt the color of flooded roads, it read TOO TOUGH TO DIE.

None of them spoke until they'd crossed the border. Jacqueline could still smell the cologne. They were all wearing it. It was in the back of her throat with the bile. She thought of them passing the bottle around, shaking it onto their palms, slapping it onto the backs of their necks, smoothing it over their cheeks. Like boys preparing for a dance.

—

SHE HAS NOT RETURNED to see the tall man who served her lunch.

Go see him, my love. Jacqueline lying on the couch, head in her mother's lap. Go see him. You've got nothing better, her mother says, stroking and stroking Jacqueline's forehead.

Jacqueline stays behind the mattress and tries to think of her sister. Tries to think of Saifa *before,* but it is impossible. There is only Saifa. You do not choose where to see her. She should not have thought of her at all. There is no separating Saifa from time.

Maybe one day, you can think of her without this, her mother says.

Jacqueline is caught now. Her sister is there and she can't stop it.

This is why you must not stand still.

But it is too late.

Again, she feels madness coming.

It stalks her on the heels of all the rest.

What else to call it?

Saifa, alone in the yellow chair. She is looking out the window, a chemistry book resting on her belly.

Saifa, sixteen, seven months pregnant. She's enormous.

They are listening to the news of their country in chaos. Government soldiers terrorizing Gbah. Executing men refusing conscription, raping girls as young as eleven, the BBC reports. The LURD rebels closer and closer to Monrovia.

When the power goes out for the fourth time in an hour the sound vanishes and her mother says, "Plug it into Saifa."

Her father hands her the cord and Saifa fits the prongs into her nostrils.

"Still doesn't work," he says. "Must be something wrong with the radio."

Go see him, her mother says. Go see him, my love. My love, she says in her very gentlest voice, the one reserved for her daughters and only when they were falling, when they could no longer understand the things that happened in a life. Lives in which, even with all their privilege, the most terrible things had begun to enter, incomprehensible to her daughters, impossible for her to explain.

My love, she says in that calmest, surest whisper, get up, go and see him.

Jacqueline, weeping, says, "Tomorrow, I'll go tomorrow, Mama."

She closes her eyes and imagines the mountain above

her, all those layers of earth and rock and ash. This is her mother's trick: Think of all the time. Think of all the people. Of every creature that has lived, that lives now. Think of all the history, of all the people that have ever lived. You are tiny. You are an eyelash, my little girl.

Jacqueline turns onto her side, draws her legs in, and presses her smooth knees against the damp back wall of the cave. She tries, but can imagine no one else, can see no other life but her own.

You are a selfish girl, her mother says.

Jacqueline shifts her body so that her hip takes more of her weight.

It is the pain of bone against rock that helps to pass time. It is the same lesson, she thinks. You must be careful of luxury. Keep a present need. Always keep a present need. Make it unbearable. Solve no problem too quickly.

She sleeps and in the morning does not remember her dreams.

When she wakes she is in shadow. The sea is bright in the low sun. She returns the mattress to its proper place and lies facedown so that she can rest her chin on her folded hands.

A yacht in full sail, white as the moon, cuts across the bay.

She watches the hours change the color of the sky.

She sleeps and dreams she is giving birth to her sister's child.

IN THE MORNING she walked along the water to the far end of the beach, where she sat on the sand with her back to the road. The first bus arrived half full. She focused on the couples, the groups of girls. People with children were never interested. She avoided the single men. She walked end to end. Twenty minutes and not a job. She waited on a bench facing the sea across the street from the gyro shop. She marked time on the Pepsi clock. Two hours. The man saw her the second time she turned to look, but he did not wave. Perhaps he felt betrayed, as if she'd broken some pact. She was sorry. She'd make it right tomorrow. She wished she had something to read. A magazine, a newspaper. Above all, a paperback. She wanted something solid to hold, to carry with her. She added it to her list.

Book followed *watch*.

The beach was crowded now. More so than she'd ever seen it. She hadn't noticed them arrive, but there they were. So many people it frightened her. Where had they come from? Those hours seemed like they'd been cut out of her life, easily extracted like two dead teeth. All she could remember of them was the idea of the paperback and the man looking at her, his elbows on the takeaway window. She hated the idea of going down to the sand. She hadn't eaten in two days. She was dizzy, but she went.

Her first job was two blond girls in bikinis.

One of them doing a headstand, the other with legs crossed, eyes closed, thumbs and forefingers joined. Both of them laughing. They took her immediately. Two five-minute foot massages. She knelt and held a foot in her hands, pushing her thumbs along the sole. It felt as if she were talking to a single person. Not a person. Something else.

"So where do you go to school?"

"Columbia."

"Wow. I didn't get in."

"Neither did I."

"We're both at Duke."

"Sophomores."

"You're a grad student?"

"Yes."

"In what?"

"Journalism." She'd decided today it would be journalism; she switched to another foot.

"Amazing. They have a great program."

"I love your accent. What are you, like, Jamaican?"

"Liberian."

"That's in Africa, right?"

Jacqueline nodded.

"You make enough money like this?"

"I stay in a hostel."

"Oh cool, us too. Which one?"

She hesitated.

"Maybe she doesn't want to say?"

"Oh my God, I'm sorry."

"Well, we're in Fira. I just asked because I thought how
random if we were staying in the same one, you know?"

"Mine's not in Fira," Jacqueline said. Then she looked
up, smiled at one of the faces, and returned to the foot.

"Are you in Oìa? I heard that's the best."

"It's nice. Very quiet."

Jacqueline had moved on to the third foot. It was too fast
probably, but they didn't protest. She ended each massage by
rubbing sand against the soles of their feet. A new flourish.
"And finally to exfoliate," she said.

"Amazing." They gave her a five-euro bill.

"Keep the change."

"You know, if you ever want to meet out for a drink, we're
here for a week more."

"Sure," she said, folding the bill in half.

One of them handed her a card.

"Call whenever."

She stood above them, brushing sand from her knees.
"Sure," she said. "Next time I'm in Fira."

She dropped the card into her skirt pocket, waved at
them, and moved on down the sand.

She thought of walking with Helen across the field after

classes in Cheltenham. The two of them sneaking cigarettes in the trees behind Glenlee. The two of them sitting side by side on the train. Half term and on their way to visit Helen's family in London.

Call, her mother said. Call.

Jacqueline saw the house on Lonsdale Road, Helen's bedroom, the wallpaper. Yellow flowers on blue.

She was lying on the deep white carpet looking up at Helen, who stood smoking at the open window in a black T-shirt. Cropped blond hair, her skinny legs, faint blue veins beneath pale skin. There was something printed on the T-shirt. A band name. A bar. Some famous face. But it wouldn't come into focus.

"JaJa," Helen said. "What are we going to *do* tonight?"

A phone call, JaJa, her mother said, a single phone call. Wouldn't they help you, my heart?

Yes, Jacqueline said, they would, and held her mother's gaze.

The money would be enough to go and see the tall man. It would provide pretext. She needed that shade. She needed to eat, but there was more than half the beach to travel. She stood up to her thighs in the water, until it passed, until some strength returned, and then she pushed along. She stayed down on the wet sand, keeping away from the building crowd, watching for customers.

There was a couple sitting quietly up at the edge of the dry sand, just before it broke away and sloped to the sea. They were on matching blue towels neatly laid out, side by side, not a corner out of place. The woman with her legs crossed, the man leaning back on his elbows.

"Excuse me for bothering you," she began with the last of her energy.

They looked up at her.

"Do you speak English?"

They both nodded.

"Oh, great. So, I'll be a student in the States this fall and

I'm traveling around Europe this summer. I support myself by giving massages and was wondering if you'd like one. If either of you would like a massage."

She reached for her visor to make certain it was straight.

"I don't know," the man said. He removed his sunglasses and squinted up at her.

"What kind of massage is it?" The woman interlaced her fingers, raised her arms above her head, and drew herself into a long graceful stretch.

"Oh, it's a traditional form." She'd replaced the word *style* with *form*. "Something my mother taught me."

The woman smiled at this. She reminded Jacqueline of a restless cat.

"Sit down," she said.

Jacqueline kneeled in the sand. She did not like to kneel, but she couldn't find a better position to do this work.

"Sure," the woman said. "Why not a massage?" She unfolded her legs and moved easily back along the towel.

"What are your rates?" The man was watching his wife point and pull her feet, which moved like little levers.

"Two euros for five minutes," she said.

He turned to her. "You live on that?" he asked.

She shrugged.

Jacqueline lifted the woman's right ankle and cradled it in her hand. It was a small foot with a high arch and clear-varnished toenails. She pressed her thumbs into the flat pad of the heel.

"You tell me if it's too hard." She held the foot steady and applied a slow, constant pressure.

"Oh. As hard as you like."

She pushed deeper.

"That's wonderful. Oh, God." She fell back and closed her eyes. "Do five minutes a foot, okay? Can you do that?"

"Of course." Plus five makes nine. She thought of the shaded table, the basket of bread.

"My wife's a glutton." She glanced over and smiled.

There was something soft about him. "How long have you been doing this?"

"Massages? About a month. Bit longer maybe."

He nodded.

"Where are you in school?"

"Columbia."

"Yeah? You like it?"

"I don't know. I start in September."

"Where are you moving from?"

"Liberia."

"Liberia?"

She slid her thumbs along the arch and began working the ball of the foot.

"When did you leave?"

"June."

Was that right? She couldn't remember.

"June," he repeated. She could feel him staring at her. "I'm glad you got out safe," he said after a long pause.

She turned to him, surprised by the tenderness in his voice.

"Thank you." She smiled. "I think your wife has fallen asleep."

"I guess you're talented."

Jacqueline's legs were going numb.

"Must be strange to go from there to here. To an island like this, to rubbing the feet of people like us."

"People like you?"

"With time to lie in the sun."

"It's not what I think about."

He seemed embarrassed.

"Why did you stay so long?"

"My father was a believer."

"In Taylor?"

She nodded.

The woman woke up and stretched her arms above her

head again, twisting slightly. "Oh," she said. "You have such lovely hands."

Jacqueline moved on to the right foot. The man watched a piece of blue sea glass as he rolled it between his fingers.

For a moment, while no one was speaking, she turned her head from side to side to stretch her neck. A few meters down the beach, thin blanket around his shoulders, the Senegalese man was watching her. He smiled. She returned to the woman's foot, counted fifteen seconds, and stopped.

"Okay," she said. Her voice was thin.

"Thank you, thank you," the woman said. "Just lovely. You don't have a card or something do you? Some way to reach you? I swear I could do this every day."

"No, I'm sorry."

"Nowhere? No phone? Nothing?"

She shook her head. She couldn't master the fear. She could feel his fingers pulling her hair, could feel it crushing the muscles in the back of her neck, fingers against vertebrae. He was striding toward her, smiling, without hesitation, so certain of himself, everything under his control.

She couldn't stand. Her legs were still numb. She did not want to wait but the blood wouldn't flow. There was only the cold tingling turning warmer.

"Here you go."

The man was holding something out to her.

"Take it," he said. "Please."

The woman was swinging her knees from side to side. "Seriously, you earned every *fucking* penny."

Jacqueline took the money into her left hand, shifted forward, slipped the bill into her pocket, stumbled, and fell back off her heels into the sand. She forced a smile. Gave a dry, horrible laugh. Protect yourself. As if she'd meant to fall. As if she were only stretching her legs out. She could not stand. She was nauseated, the sky was turning white, was turning white, was turning away from her, swelling now into white. Breathe. Breathe. Get to the water. Stand up and swim. Swim.

Then it came back. The sky. And then the surface beneath her. And then her own weight.

She sat up and smiled. The woman, eyes closed, was still moving her knees from side to side like a metronome. Left. Right. Left. Right. The man had his hand on Jacqueline's foot.

She heard the metronome ticking atop their ridiculous piano.

"You all right?"

"Fine," she said. It had felt like hours. She'd been gone so long. "Sometimes, my back spasms. Comes on fast."

"Sure," he said. "I thought, you know . . . it was as if you'd passed out."

"No."

"We'll be back. Look for us," the woman said to the sky.

The man stared with his girlish eyes.

"Thank you," she said. She looked down at her foot. His hand was still resting there. He drew it away immediately.

"You're sure you're okay?"

"Yes. Just need to get out of the sun for a bit."

She took a long breath and stood up. "Take care," she said and moved through the burning black sand in the direction of the road. She could barely see. Now it seemed impossible. Why would he be out there with a blanket around him? Had he been swimming? Was it a towel? Fabric to dry his skin. Why did it matter? So what if he'd been there? So what if he saw her? But it *did* matter. She could not be known here. Not like that. Not by them. She would say these were her friends. And the money? She was coming to get food. To bring them food. There was logic in this. It would be enough. And having the story would get her to the wall. It was taking a very long time. Then she was there at the steps, resting at the bottom, her hand on the burning steel banister. She climbed to the top and came out onto the road. The man was sitting on a bench, red beach towel wrapped around his shoulders.

"Hello, sister."

The man said it to mock her. The inflection was wrong, the words were repeated sounds, she thought, not language. Still, Jacqueline recognized that cold, arrogant, angry smile. It seemed to exist separate from the body. She was not frightened, but she knew, even then in her haze of hunger and dehydration, that she would have to leave. The man posed all threats at once. She supported herself with her hand and did not move because she did not want to fall.

"Why you're not at hotel? In other town. Why you like this beach so much?" He raised his chin.

She looked down the road past the restaurant to where the other two men, his partners, were standing behind their blankets of sunglasses. It was possible that he posed no threat at all, that he was being friendly, playful. Perhaps he meant no harm, but she did not like his face and she did not like to be identified. This was what had prevented her from returning to the restaurant, to the man who had fed her, who seemed to want nothing but to see her safe. Though this was impossible, of course. If she considered the things that people had wanted of her over the course of her life, she could use those things as a way to chart the decline of her life.

Evolution, her mother said. To chart the evolution, not the decline. There is no rise. There is no fall, there is simply what He wants of you.

"What do you want?"

"Only to say hello. To welcome you. To say to you, *bon chance,* my friend."

She looked at him. Studied his eyes, his arms spread out, his long hands hanging still across the top of the bench.

"Thank you," she said and would have walked on, but did not have the strength.

"You are doing here?"

"What?"

"On the beach. You are doing what?"

"I don't understand," she said.

He waved his hand at her like she'd told him a bad joke. "Yes," he said. "You do. You do."

Jacqueline stared at him.

"You are working."

She did not respond.

"You are working and I think you are living. Here," he said. "I am thinking you are living here."

"I'm going to have lunch," she said and pushed herself away from the railing. It was the new adrenaline that allowed her to move, adrenaline of fear, of anger.

"It is possible," he said and looked at her again with that broad cruel smile, "it is possible I know where is."

She'd taken a step forward. She would have to pass in front of him now to get to the restaurant.

"What is? Know where what is?"

"The place you are living." He nodded toward the beach.

Jacqueline stood beneath the shower, naked in the street-light.

"You can work for me," he said, the smile now absent.

"No, thank you." Jacqueline took two steps to pass the man. His long right arm came alive. He snatched her wrist in his rough hand.

She met his eyes and did not fight and did not look at the fingers on her arm. "Do not touch me," she said. He kept his hand where it was and smiled at passersby as if it were a game he and Jacqueline were playing. She did not want to be seen, did not want this attention, but she would not smile. She focused on his face, trying to work out what he was exactly, the danger he posed. There were a thousand degrees. Everything seemed to bend around her and despite the fear she felt, the adrenaline had begun to dilute and dis-appear. Perhaps there was none left. And without it fear took on a different feeling altogether. What she had left was anger, which gave her enough power to pull her arm away. People stopped to look. An incongruous scene on this quiet bay.

Jacqueline pulled hard. She felt his nails claw across her skin. She'd broken his grip and now she walked from him toward the restaurant.

She entered and took a seat at a table farthest from the sidewalk, closest to the sea. There were three raised red lines on her arm. She was very tired and more than food, more than water, what she wanted then was to sleep, was to hide away, to bury herself somewhere and close her eyes, to be contained and protected and gone.

It was a woman who brought the menu, who brought the bottle of water, the basket of bread. Jacqueline watched the door to the kitchen, but it was always the waitress who came and went.

"Is the owner here?" she asked.

"Is there a problem?"

"Not at all. No. I was just hoping to speak to him today."

"To speak to him?"

Jacqueline looked up. Until then the woman had been a vague presence, a sweeping hand, a smell of garlic and dirty oil. All familiar smells, which made her trust that presence. But the face was jarring. Somehow she'd expected a face like her mother's, or some element of her there in the eyes or in the voice. But this woman gazing down at her—pale skin, black hair—was young and looked at Jacqueline with suspicion.

"Why would you need to speak to the owner?"

"Oh, only because," she began. She wanted to say that he had helped her, that she owed him money for a meal, that she wanted to repay him today, to thank him for the water. But she understood that this must be the man's girlfriend, his wife, so she said she was hoping for a job, she wondered if there might be a job. She did not want to cause him any trouble.

"We're not hiring anyone now."

Jacqueline nodded and said she understood and ordered the yemista. When the woman left, she drank half the bottle of water before using the glass. Now her focus widened.

She ate the peppers slowly, but still her stomach cramped in tight pointed pain. It was important to repay the man. She wanted to speak to him, and as the food calmed her, slowed her heart, she hoped he'd return. But it was only the woman who moved through the restaurant, proprietary and efficient. He never came. The woman left her alone with the check. Jacqueline dug the money from her skirt pocket. There were two bills. Five euros. Then she unfolded the other. It was a fifty. Fifty euros. Charity. A donation to the victims of their pathetic little war. Victims of her father's hero. Victims of her father. Charity from those people on the sand to whom she knelt.

But why anger? Why is your first response always to be furious, always to doubt? You must see, JaJa, these things are not accidents. Those people, this money, everything is intended.

Jacqueline laid the fifty down. When her change came, she slipped a twenty beneath the receipt. She owed him nothing now.

She found the bathroom, where she sat bent over on the toilet. The cramping was worse. She thought she might vomit, but she willed it down. She could not afford to lose what she'd eaten. She knew she would need it. She wanted to stay longer behind the locked door, but she was embarrassed. She washed her face and was grateful there was no mirror above the sink. She wound several feet of toilet paper around her palm, buried it in her pocket, and left the restaurant swept with nausea. She stood out front on the sidewalk and when she counted three men standing in front of the sunglasses, she turned and walked in the other direction.

IN THE CAVE, she sat with her bare legs in the sun, calves pressed against the warm rock, and watched the boats pass. She did not want to leave. She did not want to begin again. She wanted to fight. She was not afraid, but she could only lose. There was a familiar cruelty in that man. He would come for her. He had nothing else to do.

So she sat, most of herself in shade, trying to ignore the pain in her stomach and the loss she felt for this new home. She liked the pretty bay, the changing light, her bed, the order of her life.

Nostalgia, her father said.

Maybe, Jacqueline said. And anyway, she could not risk the man's cruelty. He was not the one to fight. This salesman. This bully.

No, her mother said, pouring gin over ice, he is not the one to fight.

This is not the end, her mother said. It is no more the end than any of those Spanish beaches were the end. You must go on. God has shown you that. You see it now, my heart.

She spread her money on one of the shelves, counted and arranged it, and returned it to her pocket. She folded her blanket and clothes and pressed them down into her pack. She slid the mattress to the very back of the cave, as if she might someday return.

Despite its weight, she kept the pillow.

She swung out and slipped down, and went on.

ALONG THE ROAD she stopped in a small store and bought water and half a kilo of almonds. She bought tomatoes and figs and peaches, a loaf of bread and a block of feta, and still she had plenty of money to spare. Jacqueline turned her back to the bay. She had the intention of returning to the central town where she'd arrived and perhaps finding her way onto a ferry for Athens, or to another island, but because a police car passed by, because she saw the driver's black eyes in the rearview mirror, she turned from the main road and followed a dirt path that took her upward and as she hiked she saw that she was now climbing on the mountain that had contained her. Somewhere below was her cave.

Mostly she was alone, though sometimes when she looked up she could see figures above on the higher switchbacks. She followed tourist signs for Ancient Thera and after forty minutes of steady climbing came up onto a ridge and into the wind. From here she saw the coast extend in a long arc. In the other direction she looked down at her black beach and the flat bay. She rested and watched a sailboat move across the water and disappear around the point where the mountain came to the sea. After a few minutes she saw it come out the other side, where it began to trace the wilder coast. The expanse of all that land was a surprise and the sight of it, combined with the wind blowing her sweat cold, released some pressure, allowed her to breathe, gave her a sense of lightness. She looked at the hills sloping gently to the water, the small white houses scattered among vineyards and the farms spread out in ordered green rectangles and squares to the dark coast braided with surf. The food she carried and all the land and water beneath her provided momentary peace. The feeling was akin to those brief moments of abandon when she stood naked beneath the shower.

But the color of those farms returned her to memory. To Saifa at her side, the two of them comfortable in their chairs, the rain stopped, the dark clouds moving south like great trucks. The two of them looking out at the jungle encompassing the city, more threatening than ever, the shanties on the beach, blue tarps drawn tight, the ocean turning to green marble, the ocean returning to steel. Saifa holding a radio in her hands as if it were her child, balancing it on her belly, its long silver antenna extending nearly to the overhanging roof. The two of them quiet, listening to the voice of DJ Lobo Courtnoy as he read for the Red Cross. She remembered names and that he spoke them twice before declaring each child's sex. The lilt in his voice, the unintentional poetry, accidental music in the litany of names: Patrick Tilla. Patrick Tilla. Patrick is a boy. Age three. Mother's name Mani Tilla. Father's name Jalla Tilla. Patrick Tilla, Patrick Tilla. Jonah Tilla, Jonah Tilla. Jonah is a boy. Age six. Mother's name, Mani Tilla, Father's name Jalla Tilla. Jonah Tilla. Jonah Tilla.

SHE HIKED THE LAST SECTION of the path, which ran out toward the sea and then descended into the ruins of the ancient city, where there were broken foundations, dwellings, remnants of an amphitheater, and smooth black stone-cobbled streets.

A tour bus arrived, and soon there were more people wandering the pathways, holding up maps, comparing drawings of the original city to the remains. For a while Jacqueline watched a heavy man in leather sandals recounting history while he wiped sweat and errant strands of blond hair from his forehead. But she did not listen.

Instead she leaned against a cypress tree and watched a small girl in a green dress ignore the tour guide and, balancing on a boulder, extend her arms and spread her fingers to catch the wind. A lizard came to rest on a jagged, lichen-covered stone. It snapped its tongue and then disappeared over the cliff edge.

The branches of the cypress moved above her and Jacqueline saw the place as a living city: people in the streets, smell of fresh bread, children running past, sound of bare feet on black stone, women walking together, wood smoke on wind.

She walked away from the tour group, past a man with a boy on his shoulders, past a woman in a wide, pink-banded straw sun hat.

She found the remnants of the amphitheater. Here she sat in the shade of a tall cedar. Breaking a piece of feta from the block, wetting her fingers, Jacqueline pressed it into a piece of bread. She bit pieces from a tomato, made a crude sandwich, and ate. She liked the acid in her mouth, the sharpness cutting something open in her.

She had been sleeping somewhere down below, somewhere beneath where she was now. Somewhere inside this mountain, this great hunk of earth and rock, she had been hidden away. Somewhere beneath where she was now were her shelves, her mattress, the sand her feet had carried up into the cave, the oil from her skin staining the rock, all of it already distant, remainders, remnants of a former life. Far off and otherworldly.

This is something you must learn, her mother said. The physical home is nothing. The sooner you learn that, my heart, my proud girl, so sure of yourself, so sure of your body, such confidence in the ground beneath you, the sooner you learn that, the sooner you learn that, well, her mother said, well.

Well, what?

But she knew.

It was a beautiful amphitheater. Better now, she thought, with only the lizards crossing the stage, with only the white-caps, the occasional sailboat, a hydrofoil, in the channel far below for scenery.

She imagined an audience. She imagined life returned here.

Ghosts.

But you don't believe in ghosts, her mother said. Spirits. Child of logic. No such thing.

No.

And where has all that got you? Sitting here alone. Not a pot to piss in. No one to talk to, your chest empty.

Jacqueline shook her head and stood up. She finished the bottle of water, returned the food to her pack.

If not, then what is left? What is memory, if not ghosts?

The problem is not ghosts, the problem now is what to do next.

But her mother said nothing.

Jacqueline turned to watch the group of tourists follow the blond man into the amphitheater.

She left the ruins and followed the fall line into a stand of gnarled, stubborn-looking cypress trees. Their rough branches fanned out to screen the wind blowing harder up the coast. She dropped her pack here and sat on the ground softened by fragrant fallen needles. Through the branches she could look back and spy on the tourists moving up and down the streets.

She had clear views north and west. Otherwise she was cupped in by the curving trees. An amphitheater of her own. She noticed the sun and was surprised to find it so low.

Time passes, her mother said, peeling carrots. No matter what you do. No matter what happens, she said, crushing garlic, hammering the side of her favorite knife with her fist.

Beauty or horror, my heart. Turning on the stove. Beauty or horror, it passes.

Jacqueline saw herself sitting on the earth, watched herself rotating away from the sun.

From the terrace, she and Saifa strained their necks. They chased after it, off the terrace, onto the grass, and all the way to the property line. They jumped up and up and up.

Drowned it again, Saifa said.

Jacqueline had preferred to feel the earth, rather than pretend the sun was setting. The turning was magic enough.

She'd always wanted to follow it in a boat, stay right behind, maintain just that speed. Keep the sun right on the horizon, never let it set.

At the equator, the earth moves at one thousand miles per hour, my love, her father said, hand covering the mouthpiece of the telephone, kissing her forehead.

Just before this sunset, Jacqueline imagined taking Saifa's hand and chasing across the concrete.

Underfoot, the low-cut, dry grass. Running to the line where everything turned to wild undergrowth. The whole world pausing, settling. A deflation, a drop in pressure. Last bit of palm oil leaving the funnel. The sun flattening out. The flares, the ocean going dark, the lights snapping on across Monrovia, cooking fires appearing between the blue tarps on the beach.

She wrapped herself in the blanket. She turned on her side and was grateful for the pillow. The wind pushed hard through the trees. She watched the land below, a wide, black tongue.

The lights came on across the island.

There was no moon yet to pick up the thick rope of surf, to distinguish topography, to turn the sea to tin.

She lay with her hands squeezed between her knees and stared into the night. Like this she fell asleep and dreamed the air smelled of smoke, of dried fish, of storm clouds, her mouth filled with the metallic taste of blood, everything on fire, but there was no light, the flames colorless, nothing moved, the smell unbearable, smell of burning fish and sweat, of garbage. Jacqueline couldn't breathe.

She heard the beat of rubber sandal against damp heel.

Peel and slap, peel and slap, peel and slap.

When she opened her eyes her heart was hammering in her chest. She could taste the smoke. The moon hung nearly full above a long knifing ridge.

The sea was silver.

The island was blue.

Her mouth was full of blood.

She stayed there on her side until the restlessness was too much. The wind had gone dead. Unable to sleep, she pulled herself up and walked down toward the cliff edge, where she squatted and urinated with her back to the setting moon.

She ran her tongue over the hole she'd bitten from the inside of her mouth.

The flap of skin moved free.

She worried it as she walked the ruins. The sky blued to the east, paling at the horizon. She walked every street. She slipped beneath the ropes and stood in the best-preserved dwellings. In one, she sat on the floor with her back to the wall and watched the stars as they were drawn out of the sky. She returned to the amphitheater and sat for a while. She tried to breathe deliberately, tried to keep her hands still, tried to let her tongue lie motionless in her mouth.

She stood and walked to the southern side. From here she could see the black beach. She tried to find the restaurant, but couldn't be sure which was his.

She should return there. Find the tall man with his menus.

But for what?

She shook her head.

Now you are here, she thought. You cannot return. You cannot think in terms of return. There is only away.

Forward, her mother said.

"Away," Jacqueline said. This time speaking the word.

Forward, her mother said again.

Away.

They're not the same thing, one of them said. Jacqueline wasn't sure whom.

The morning came in fast.

You'll burn your eyes, my heart.

Jacqueline turned away. Her shadow stretched long.

The whole ruined city was hers. She walked the streets again, one after the other, up and down, back and forth.

She would name them.

Jacqueline thought of the lagoon at high tide. Even if it was no longer safe then, they swam. They were alone, no cars in the sandy lot, a heavy, windless day. The two of them up to their necks in water. Their father at work, their mother at church.

She would name them. Like any city. Streets named for the dead.

Her mother stood with her arms crossed and shook her head. She added more gin to her glass. More ice. This is no place to stop.

For a while. Just for a while.

She returned to her bed, where she ate a breakfast of almonds, and watched the sun light up the island. There were towns just below and also far away. A red plastic candy wrapper blew past and floated from the cliff.

Again, the same question: What to do next?

Away from town she was safer, but there was nothing here. No water, no food, barely any shelter. Somewhere there must be a spring, she thought. Once, there must have been a well.

This is no place to stay, her mother said again, impatient. Well or no well.

Jacqueline closed her eyes. The sun was cutting the back of her neck now. She could see her mother's fingers moving along a banister, could hear the wedding band clicking against wood. Why the fingers? She tried to see a face instead, but she could not. There was the smell of the house, her mother's body cutting through the cold, filtered air, descending. Long body, tight skirt to her knees, heels, fingers, nails painted pink, and that ring clicking against the wood.

Where was the face?

The face was blurred and imprecise. But the voice was sharp as a blade.

There is nothing here but ghosts.

And they were back where they started. But it was true, there was nothing there. A ragged memorial. Useless beauty. She would have to leave. Soon. But for a while, she would stay. A few days to think it through.

She sat in her bed scooping dry needles into her hand and letting them fall through her fingers. She watched the black road slithering up the mountainside. If trouble were to come, it would come from this side, not from the trail. Here danger would arrive by car, not by foot, not in the dirt the way she'd come.

This vantage point reminded her of Monrovia, of their house.

"That haven of sophistication," her mother had said, picking lint from her skirt.

Her mother had come to visit her at Cheltenham, to see Jacqueline's boardinghouse, to wander the campus. To see what their dirty money had paid for, her daughter's ordered and peaceful life, the pristine lawns, the immovable stone buildings, the silent library. They visited Christ Church in Lansdown, where they'd sat together in a back pew holding hands in the dim light. Jacqueline was fifteen.

"Stay here," her mother had said. "Now. After you graduate. No matter what your father says. No matter what he offers you. No matter his promises. Never come home. Promise me, JaJa. Promise me."

Jacqueline could smell the gin mingling with the sweetness of her mother's perfume.

Shalimar.

"I promise," she said.

"We'll come to you, okay? We'll visit. No matter how lonely you are, whatever your father says about Taylor, and his peace deal, and what he'll do for the country and our glorious future. Whatever he says, never come home. Do you understand me? Never."

"Yes," Jacqueline said. "I promise."

"Good," her mother said, breathing hard now through her open mouth. "Good."

———

THE WIND BLEW ACROSS the ruins and Jacqueline watched her father's left hand move across the shining black lacquered top of the grand piano no one could play.

A huge hand.

Heavy and thick.

She felt its weight, the wedding band gold and immovable.

It lay in her two hands, lifeless until Saifa called "Crab" and then it danced and skittered up Jacqueline's arm and onto her head and down her back and over her knees. It pinched her toes until she laughed all the breath from her body. Me, now, Saifa screamed, Me.

And the crab came to rest on her shoulder, heavy and still.

Jacqueline shook her head.

What could be more absurd than a piano?

HERE DANGER WOULD COME UP THE ROAD. No band of lunatic children would rise dead-eyed from the jungle.

No, the danger would come in a car. It would be civilized. It would be uniformed. It would be clean.

What *was* the danger? What would her father say? He had once said that danger is not the point. What do you want? That's the only question. Danger is only the obstacle to that thing. It must be irrelevant to your desire.

In this way, her mother said, turning her back on them, your father is the worst of men.

And not only in this way, Jacqueline thought.

A long tour bus the color of dry blood turned and began to rise up the road. She could hear the stuttering downshift. She watched it come slow around the sharpest hairpin and then disappear. She stood and adjusted her pack. When the bus came back into view, she swept the needles from her skirt and, leaving the pillow behind, began to walk the streets where she would play curious tourist.

She would try to see herself in their expressions. What was she? She took a swig of water. Then she wet her hands and smoothed it over her neck, her forehead. She wiped the crust from the corners of her eyes, patted her cheeks. She drew herself up into a posture of confidence, brought her face into a smile.

She stood at the very entrance to the ruins and waited until the bus came sweeping into the parking lot. The doors opened and people spilled out, shielding their eyes, adjusting their hats, and stretching their backs. The sound of voices rose up to Jacqueline, who listened intently.

A small woman in a white polo shirt marched up from

the parking lot. She was holding a pink umbrella high above her head. The tourists followed.

"Well, you're here early."

Jacqueline turned and brought the smile into place.

"I'm usually the first one up. My trademark."

Jacqueline nodded. "I've never been."

The woman's pale charges began to arrive, but she ignored them.

"You came up the trail?"

"It's a beautiful walk."

"You're welcome to come along." The woman smiled. SANTOTOUR was embroidered in red thread across her right breast. "No charge."

"Are you sure?"

"You're up here alone?"

She nodded and then added, "My husband's at the pool."

The woman smiled. "Men are so dull."

Jacqueline forced a laugh. The speaking required such energy.

"Well, come along with us?"

"Thank you," she said and stepped aside as the woman turned to the group.

"You are all now standing at the entrance of what was once the city of Thera," the woman said, driving the point of her umbrella into the dirt between her feet.

The group, sluggish in the early morning, quieted.

"This is Mesa Vouno mountain, three hundred and sixty meters above the sea. And here, where we're all standing now, began a street nearly eight hundred meters long. Up there to the right was a garrison. Across from the theater there"—she extended her arm and everyone looked—"was the residential section of the city, which included a lovely agora. And down there was a small temple. All of the buildings were constructed with the local limestone you see around you. Far below us, there to the north where the city of Kamari is today, was once a great necropolis."

Jacqueline was close to the tour guide and could smell her perfume. She envied the silver earrings, the clean shirt, the smooth tan legs.

"We'll walk down in this direction here." Up went the umbrella. As they walked, Jacqueline kept close.

"The great historian Herodotus wrote about Thera and its mythical Spartan ruler, Theras, for whom, obviously, this city and the island itself were both named. Santorini, or Saint Irene, was a name given to the island by the Latin Empire, but the official Greek name is Thera. Later, in the third century BC, there's evidence of a whole navy stationed in what was once a great harbor down below. And until the fifth century, it was the only settlement on the entire island."

They stopped before one of the better-preserved houses, where there was a single Doric column and a perfectly flat bench.

"The fact is, before I go on about Thera, and many of you must know this already, the real archeological magic here is Akrotiri. You should all see it. So let me talk about that a bit as well. But first, how many of you have seen the caldera?"

All of them raised their hands. Jacqueline followed suit.

"And Nea Kameni?"

Silence.

"Nea Kameni is the island in the middle of the caldera."

Several people raised their hands.

"Well, you should all go down. Go on a calm day. Nea Kameni is a volcano. Still alive. It wasn't even there a few hundred years ago, and then, seventeen something, up it comes right out of the water. Now you can climb to the top of it. Right in the middle of all that water, it's like a wasteland out there."

"You mean it could still erupt?" someone asked.

Those who were staring off at the sea returned their attention to the tour guide.

"Well, it erupted in 1950. Then there was an earthquake

in 1956. Destroyed everything. People left forever, deserted their villages."

"So, it could still erupt?"

"Sure," the tour guide said. "And what it is now is just what was left after that first eruption."

"Really?"

"Listen, imagine you're Minoans. You live in Akrotiri. A real city. A famous city. Some people say that it was Plato's Atlantis. A city with streets, squares, buildings, paintings, running water, hot and cold by the way, boats for fishing, boats for pleasure. It made this place look like a highway rest stop."

Someone laughed.

"Go see it. It's all preserved. Incredible. And this was *before* the Greeks. Thousands of years before. Medicine. The women ate saffron crocus when they had cramps. There were antelopes. Dolphins. A city in its prime. And then one day, the island explodes and everyone, every single person, is killed. The center of the island just turns to ash and vanishes into the air. Nothing of it is left. Everything gone. The eruption sets off a tsunami that rolls out and crushes Crete, the very center of Minoan culture. After thousands of years the Minoans vanish from history. Cities, palaces, naked acrobats. Gone. And it's not just Thera or Akrotiri, the whole island is a ruin. This? What's known to you as Santorini? It's just what's left of an island."

Two young boys stared at the tour guide. They were twins, each dressed in matching clothes—red sneakers, khaki shorts, white T-shirts painted with the Greek flag, white baseball caps.

The tour guide turned to the dwelling and said, "Anyway, this is where people lived. Try to imagine it."

Then they made their way down nearer to the edge of the cliff.

"Here," she said, pointing with the umbrella to a knot of rock on the mountain ridge, "was a grotto dedicated to

Hermes and Heracles. Hermes, god of merchants, thieves, and oratory. Heracles, or to the Romans, Hercules. And here lived the officers in peristyle houses with nothing between them and these views, whereas the rest of the people, the riffraff, they lived up the mountain there."

She looked at Jacqueline for a moment and then went on, "Not nearly as interesting as Akrotiri, or as beautiful as the caldera, but they did discover dedications on altar stones dating all the way from the ninth to eighth centuries, which is to say the oldest known examples of the Greek alphabet. So here we are, in the very heart of human civilization—Greece. On the other hand, those same dedications make reference to pederasty. Anyway, if you'd like to venture on and wander around a bit, you're welcome. Please be very careful with your trash, and don't go beyond the roped-off sections. We'll be heading back soon."

She handed out small maps of the ruins and the people dispersed.

"It was probably nicer up here without us," the woman said.

Jacqueline smiled. "No, it was interesting."

Neither of them spoke for a moment. Jacqueline wanted to stay and talk.

"The island just blew up?" she asked.

They'd begun to walk and now the tour guide climbed up onto a boulder, and Jacqueline followed her. They sat. The woman dug around in her purse and withdrew a pack of gum. She offered a piece. Jacqueline put it in her mouth and chewed. The sweetness was dizzying.

"Can you imagine?"

"I was thinking of the sound."

The woman glanced at her and then back to the coastline.

Jacqueline didn't continue. She wasn't sure if she'd spoken the sentence aloud.

"I'd never thought about the sound," the woman said. "But you're right, it would have been awful. The world tearing up from beneath your feet. It's always the buildup that's worse. Imagine how frightening to hear that. Whatever the sound, it would have been coming from the ground. Like some kind of monster. It's always the suspense that kills you."

Jacqueline nodded and kept her eyes on the water.

"I'm Callie," the tour guide said, offering her hand.

"Jacqueline."

It was a strong handshake. Solid. And she felt a start, the body's impulse to cry, which surprised her, and which she tamped down and put away.

They were sitting side by side, with their feet drawn up. The tour guide leaned back on her palms. Jacqueline remained forward, her arms draped around her knees. She knew that the woman had seen her feet—the dead skin, the calluses rough and thick, the broken nails. The feet of a vagrant.

"So, where are you staying Jacqueline?"

This question again.

"In Oìa," she said, looking at the discolored nail of her right big toe.

"Ah, the most beautiful."

So she'd heard. Jacqueline smiled and then to change the subject, she asked, "Are you Greek?"

"American. My husband is Greek. From Thessaloniki, but we live in Athens."

"Are you a tour guide in Athens too?"

"Yes," the woman said, as if disappointed by her answer.

Jacqueline felt safe there talking to this woman, having a conversation just the two of them, looking out over the towns below. She had the impulse then to explain her feet, to make clear that she was not a vagrant.

Is that not what you are? Are you not exactly that? And so what if you are? There is no shame in *that*. There is no shame in seeking the kindness of strangers, my heart. No, the shame lies elsewhere.

Jacqueline shook her head and saw the tour guide look at her from behind her sunglasses.

Graceless coward. Prideful coward, there is no room for it. We are not concerned with your dignity, we are concerned with your survival, with your progress, and then, perhaps, with your peace.

Jacqueline leaned back to match the posture of the tour guide.

As to whether or not we trust this woman, her mother said, drying her hands on a red-and-white-checked dish towel, one isn't to be reckless. One isn't to be reckless, she said and walked from the kitchen toward the bedroom, where she would undress, slip a clear plastic cap over her head, and step beneath the shower. There were parties that evening.

"Where are you from?"

"Liberia."

"East Africa?"

"West."

"West, right. I'm sorry."

"Don't be. We're very small."

"Charles Taylor?"

"Yes."

"I'm sorry," the tour guide said. "I know so little about it."

"Don't be silly," Jacqueline said, waving her hand as if she were batting away a moth.

The woman kicked her sandals off and stretched her feet out in front of her. Each nail neatly painted the palest pink.

A man's pride shall bring him low: but honor shall uphold the humble in spirit. Proverbs, her mother said, standing before her wide closet. We were a *civilized* family. But we were never prideful.

Jacqueline knew this to be a barefaced lie, but held her tongue. Hypocrite, she wanted to say. Liar. Coward yourself.

My heart, her mother said. Love. What's important now is to determine who to trust, what to eat, where to sleep, how to live. To work out the problem of what is next.

Jacqueline thought of the two small egrets that wandered the lawn behind the house. She saw them stepping cautiously through the grass, their long necks curling and straightening like snakes. So careful that Saifa called them the tiptoe birds.

It was becoming more and more difficult to distinguish between what was happening and what had happened. What was memory and what was not.

The tour guide was speaking.

"Sorry?" Jacqueline said.

"I just wondered where you were staying."

"Oh, we rented a little place. An apartment."

"That's great. Which one? I know so many people on the island."

"I can't remember the woman's name. My husband took care of it."

"I see, and you're here from Liberia? Vacationing?"

There was a touch of accusation, of mistrust, Jacqueline thought.

"We live in New York. You know, we're of the lucky classes."

"Sorry to ask so many questions."

"I don't mind."

But she had begun to mind. With every answer she was putting herself further into danger. She could already tell the woman didn't trust her, was investigating, making assessments. She was angry. Both because of what she perceived as this woman's arrogance and because of her own weakness—to respond the way she had, to let that irritation show, that acid. It was undisciplined of her, weak, and it would only make her more vulnerable. You must be graceful and kind. You must be elegant and demure. You must be confident without ever being haughty. You must always, always be deferential. As if everyone you meet is holding a rifle to your throat.

She sat up, stepped from the boulder, and stretched her

arms above her head. She was weak with hunger, but didn't want to reveal her strange picnic—the feta might have gone off from the heat, the bread crushed, the tomatoes bruised. She wanted to be alone, to assemble her lunch, to sit in the shade of her cypress trees. She did not want to have to answer any further questions, or see this woman's toes, or her oiled knees.

"Well," she said, but then didn't finish her sentence. She couldn't say that she was leaving, that she had somewhere to be. If she did she'd have to walk in the direction of that place and there was no place. The only place she could go with confidence was the black beach below and she didn't have the energy for that—not for the walk down, and not for the danger, which she was sure lay in wait.

"I suppose I should get my group together. You're welcome to come along. Free ride down."

"No," Jacqueline said, practicing that casual stretch she'd learned from the women on the beach. Ease of leisure. Body at peace. Alert to nothing. Everything in the background. Eyes closed. Sun on skin. Changing light.

"No, I think I'll wander around up here a while, but thank you. For the offer, for the tour. I should pay you," she said and smiled, this time looking directly at her, daring her to accept.

"It's nothing." The tour guide extended her hand and smiled as if she were indulging the fantasies of a child.

They shook hands and the pressure of that woman's grip caused such a fluttering agitation that she turned away.

"You really like it up here, don't you?"

There it was again, that quiet note of condescension, of suspicion. It *was* suspicion, wasn't it? It made her furious and yet she was so shaken by the simple pressure of a hand in hers. She was paralyzed by the two emotions. Anger and what? She did not know.

"I do," she said. "It's very peaceful."

"It really is. Among all these ghosts. Well, we're up here every morning through the summer. Maybe I'll see you again.

And here's a card, if you and your husband ever want a private tour, give me a call."

"Sure," Jacqueline said, convinced she was being mocked.

"Take care of yourself," the tour guide said, waved, raised the umbrella, and went about rounding up her charges. Obediently they followed her down to the parking lot, where the bus sat alone on the black asphalt, the driver standing by the open door, smoking a cigarette in the sun. Far below, Jacqueline could see another bus beginning to make its way up the road.

"You don't believe even in a spirit?" Saifa asked.

Jacqueline had graduated and was home from England. Eighteen years old. Her father had invented a job for her and she'd returned, breaking her promise. My little minister of tourism. What timing, he'd said on the telephone. Ghankay president at last, and you with your expensive diploma. Come home and you will see. Everything has changed, my love. Do you know what he says? He wants Liberia to be the Hong Kong of West Africa! Come home and see it.

Even across the ocean she could see him beaming, so full of pride and stupid faith.

So she came home.

And in the mornings the car arrived, her father held the door for her, and together they rode along Randall Street, and through the gates of the Executive Mansion, where she had a small office with a desk and a window.

And a green telephone.

I'm calling from the ministry of tourism, sir. We'd like to invite you to come visit our country. Our new country. You've never seen such beaches. A secret paradise, sir. And Bomi Lake. Also known as the Blue Lake. A national treasure. You've never seen such colors. And our tropical forests. And English, sir, we all speak English. And President Taylor would be happy to cover costs. But why not write about the *future*, sir? Why not write about that? This is not the old Liberia. This is President Charles Taylor's Liberia, sir.

Day after day in her business suits. Jacqueline clicking along the hallways to her neat little office. And the evenings drinking with the journalists and the UN workers at the Mamba Point Hotel.

Have you seen these beaches? Why not write about the future? No, the war is over, sir. The war is over.

Yes, her mother said. Why not write about that? What did you promise me, little liar? Never come home, I said. Never come home, you promised.

"You believe in nothing, JaJa?" Saifa had come to look so much like their father. Her cheeks fatter now, the same smile, the same bright eyes.

Jacqueline shook her head. "No, not even in a spirit."

"So what are we then?"

"Flesh and water. What do you think we are?"

Jacqueline home with the arrogance of someone who imagines she's seen the world.

But it was Saifa who'd seen the world. Little Saifa, educated at home, by tutors until the tutors vanished, by the radio, by what she saw out the windows of their car.

"But what's the thing that keeps us alive? Even if there's no God, there's a spirit in us. Something like that?"

Jacqueline shook her head again. "We are our bodies, and we are memory. That's it. That's spirit. That's God."

"What do you mean?"

"You know what I mean."

Saifa looked away.

Jacqueline couldn't resist taunting her sister, couldn't resist torturing her by using the veil of truth telling. "We're all going to die."

Now she regretted it.

"You don't know," Saifa said.

Their mother was in the kitchen arranging white pepper flowers in a glass vase the color of dry palm fronds.

Their father was upstairs in his office.

"I know. And when you have children and *you* die, you'll

be left in *their* memory. And when I die, you'll keep me in your memory and that's the only way there's God. That's it. No matter what she tells you."

Jacqueline had nodded her head toward the kitchen, where their mother was humming "Who Are You Baby."

"Why do you get to die first?"

"I'm the oldest, SaiSai. Because I'm the oldest."

HER MOTHER WAS LOOKING out the window from the backseat of the black Mercedes. The engine was running, the air conditioner was humming. She was waiting for her husband with her wide sunglasses on.

"Not once has he been dressed before me. Not once," her mother said, sucking her teeth in irritation, straining to see herself in the rearview mirror, pursing her lips.

And then they both turned and watched as he came out of the house, smirk on his face, black leather loafers shined. He was sliding the gold Rolex over his hand, spreading his fingers to drop it into place. The coconut palms were bending and hissing in the hard wind and just then she could hear her mother make a quiet, familiar sound—sigh of love, sigh of appreciation, of helplessness, of disapproval.

And then he was in the car.

Do you see, my heart? The only things that remain atop this mountain are those things that cannot be blown away.

Jacqueline shook her head in irritation. Clichés. Truisms.

And I am one of them.

You are one of them, her mother said. Snide little girl. Arrogant shit. You are one of them.

You've said the same about places that have been obliterated. People too.

You make a choice, her mother said.

What kind of answer is that?

But she was gone. And in that moment, Jacqueline understood that she wanted one thing.

She wished not to be alone.

The sunlight was a pale orange cobweb spread across the island. The beauty of that view was unavoidable. The sheer vastness of it. The sun changing shape as it entered the water—contracting and expanding. Saint Irene was radiant, was burning. The far islands were shuddering silhouettes, purple and black and infinite.

Because of the spectacle and the beauty, because of the terror of the coming dark, in spite of herself and in spite of reason, she began to pray.

She prayed. Not for her father. Not for her mother. Not for Bernard. Not for Saifa.

She prayed for company and she prayed for the capacity to endure company.

Then she watched the sun disappear. She tried not to blink. She tried to imagine the earth moving. She tried to imagine riding its great back. She pressed her hands flat against the ground. She kept her eyes on the sun and swore she could feel the world taking her, hurtling away as the sky at the horizon burst and divided into orange and blue, pink and yellow, and then little by little everything went dark and Jacqueline began to cry.

She was thinking of the way she used to walk into parties.

OVER THE FOLLOWING DAYS she waited until the tour guide had come and gone. The woman was predictable—always arriving when the sun was a hand's distance from the far mountains. Later, when the other buses came, no one seemed to notice Jacqueline and she felt free to wander the ruins, or sit in the amphitheater, or, most often, lie in the shade of her cypress trees watching the landscape change color.

She paid attention to the way the wind rose and fell with the passing day. She tried to understand what it meant when the far sea took on white caps, what the sunset colors meant, what it was that drove the lizards scurrying across the rocks.

She was beginning to learn the island's language. She weighed that idea and was sure there was no madness in it. It was a kind of intimacy, but the other? That she was being received? This suggested a madness to which she could not commit. Not yet.

She did not believe it to be true. It was a fantasy, but it was becoming powerful—this notion that she was in communication with the island. Perhaps it came from spending so many hours watching it. Perhaps it came from keeping her face pressed so close to the ground, her hands in the needles, her feet in the dirt of it, her body so exposed to its ever-present wind. There was solace in this.

But whatever it meant, it was also true that she had begun to believe that somewhere far out below her, somewhere along that ridge, along the shore, beyond her to the north, something was receiving her thoughts. That someone was listening. No, not listening. Not listening, but receiving, absorbing, responding to her somehow.

And talking to me is not madness, my love? How is one thing madness and the other thing not? What do you call the other thing, by the way? I don't remember. What do you call it? Reason? Logic? Sanity? Idiot girl.

The difference is clear. It is not the same, because you are memory. The other is something else entirely.

I see, her mother said, gazing at her over the tops of her reading glasses. The smirk had softened. The expression was no longer superior, no longer one of bemusement. It had become something else, something containing sadness. She was sitting in the brown leather chair. She was reading something, but Jacqueline could not see what. There was a glass on a coaster. Gin and tonic water and the juice of a whole lime over ice.

Do you see the distinction? There's a difference. A tremendous difference between recollection and madness.

Her mother said nothing.

What was there on that mountain was what was left, what had not been blown away, exploded, shaken free, or burned. The blocks of limestone. The lizards. The cypress trees.

———

SHE WAS ACUTELY AWARE OF CHANGING LIGHT, but not the chain of days. After a certain amount of time she was surprised to discover there were only a few almonds left. A little water.

She thought there might be a certain dignity in this kind

of death. In riding the earth away from the sun, through the moonlight, steadily breaking down, depriving herself of nourishment, dying there in the wind on the mountain. There would be a dignity in that, a dignity in the decision.

And while she thought, her mother watched. Jacqueline saw her somewhere she could not place, in a room she did not know, with a gentle expression she did not recognize.

Jacqueline waited.

She looked out across the island and time became passing colors. The ground shifted and turned beneath her. There were noises she did not recognize. The moon was brighter than the sun. She spoke and believed she was heard. The sky seemed to thicken. Far below her, drowning in moonlight, the vineyards, the farms, broke in half and broke in half again and again and divided into pieces she believed she could carry with her.

When she woke she was exhausted and thirsty and her head beat with sharp pain. She forced herself upright and sat with her back against a tree. She emptied her pack at her feet and took inventory. She would have to leave this place. She did not want to die.

SHE PUSHED HER PILLOW to the bottom of the pack and folded the blanket and laid it on top. She wore one of the two long skirts, one of the three tank tops, one of the two bras, one of the two pairs of underwear. The rest she folded in around the blanket. The blue rubber sandals were side by side on the brown needles. The visor she wore pulled down over her eyes. She kept the tube of ChapStick in the left pocket of her skirt. She slid the empty bottle into the top of the pack and pulled the drawstring to close the main compartment. Along with her toothbrush wound with pink toilet paper and her passport, there were twenty-seven euros in the small zippered front pocket.

After she stood and slipped her feet into her sandals and hoisted the pack onto her back, there was nothing left of her here. The place had been something, had mattered in a way that the cave had not. She had an impulse to kick her foot through the needles, break the evidence of her bed, but she left it.

It was a small thing, but she left it there.

Her slight impression in the earth.

Jacqueline turned and came out from the shelter of her cypress blind. She made her way through the ruins and found her place high in the amphitheater. She was weak, but she was calm.

She had made a decision.

———

THE BUS CAME UP THE HILL and hissed to a stop in the parking lot. Soon Jacqueline saw the top of the pink umbrella moving through the air. And then there was the woman— bright-eyed and polished. Like a washed car, Jacqueline thought. The sound of the voice, though not the words, came through the air. And then there was the group assembling at the edge of the amphitheater.

So now you trust this woman with the shiny knees?

When she drank too much, her mother spit to punctuate her sentences.

"Hush," Jacqueline said aloud. "Please," she whispered. "Please be quiet."

"Jackie," the woman called and pointed her umbrella at her as if it were a sword.

"Hello," Jacqueline said when the woman arrived, black hair fallen about her shoulders.

"Thought I might find you up here again." She sat down so that they were side by side.

"It is a beautiful place."

"It is, it is, but there are other places so much more beautiful."

"You think?"

"Oìa for one, yes. Hard to imagine that you'd come here from there. I think Oìa is the most beautiful place I've ever been."

"In the world?" Jacqueline turned and looked at her.

"In the world, yes, absolutely. More beautiful than anywhere I've ever been."

Jacqueline liked the woman's eyes when she said this.

"Don't you think so?"

"I don't know," she said, which, she thought, was at least the truth.

"Well, sometimes a place just strikes a person."

"Is that where you stay when you're here?"

"No, I wish. But no. We have a house in Imerovigli. I stay there. Have you been? It's also very pretty, but no, not the same."

Jacqueline shook her head.

"Well, you should come. Have a glass of wine one night. Bring your husband."

"You're very nice."

"Oh, not all that nice. Maybe just a little bored," she said.

"Bored?"

"It's a small island."

Good, her mother said. Now you're an entertainment.

Jacqueline smiled.

"What's funny?"

She shook her head.

"Tell me. Go on."

Somehow, in that moment, the woman reminded her of Saifa—her belligerent enthusiasm, her relentless cheer.

She was having trouble keeping the tour guide's face in focus, and yet she began to laugh and couldn't stop herself. She became dizzy and, afraid she might be sick, hung her head between her knees.

"Are you okay?"

Jacqueline shook her head, but couldn't speak. For a moment everything went black. When her vision returned she was still in the same position—elbows on her knees, head in her hands.

"Are you all right?"

"Fine, fine, fine."

"It's just you went very still there for a bit. Have some of this. Here." She held out a small plastic water bottle and crackled it to get Jacqueline's attention.

The noise was very loud. She took the bottle and finished it. Then she raised her head. "I'm sorry, I forgot to eat breakfast and didn't drink enough water, I guess."

The woman moved her hand up and down Jacqueline's spine, pausing between vertebrae, as if she were examining her.

"Are you okay?" Now she spoke in a lower register, a quieter voice of tenderness. "*Mana mou,*" she said. "Why don't we go find some shade."

Jacqueline nodded. She'd begun to feel nauseated again. There is no danger in shade, she said to her mother, who shook her head and held her tongue.

The woman took Jacqueline's elbow and helped her up. They stood still together. The wind had died and she was very hot.

Then they began to walk.

If she kept her head down, and did not speak, and relied

on this woman's steady arm, she could follow her feet. And like this they made their way. But instead of finding a place beneath a tree, the woman guided Jacqueline down the hill toward the parking lot. She took her up the steps and into the bus and put her in a seat of such extraordinary comfort that there in the cool shelter she closed her eyes and began to cry. The pleasure was shocking—the velour covering against her legs, absence of wind and noise, the steady stream of cool air.

Then she heard the low hum of the idling engine. She had been elsewhere. No lingering image remained, only heat and fear and exhaustion. Now she could feel the bus trembling beneath her and the woman—Callie, Jacqueline remembered her name—was sitting at her side offering a thick square of chocolate.

"Have this," Callie said. "Take it." She was holding it out to Jacqueline as if she intended to feed it to her.

Jacqueline took the chocolate between two fingers.

"*Merci*," she whispered automatically and ate.

Merci, her mother mimicked, shaking her head in disgust.

That seat was the first blow, the chocolate the second. She was powerless. She ate and ate. There were nuts in it. There were raisins. She ate and then after some time passed she could breathe, she could see.

"Better?" Callie asked, smiling.

"Yes, thank you," Jacqueline said, and rested the side of her head against the glass. "You're very nice. I'm sorry. I don't know what's happening to me. I'm not used to this heat, or all the walking." She turned her head and looked away onto the parking lot.

"Happens all the time," Callie said, patting Jacqueline's knee.

Jacqueline didn't respond. Now that she'd recovered her mind, now that the shaking had let up, she was embarrassed and angry.

"Why do you think I keep this chocolate on the bus? People are always passing out on me."

"Thank you. I really am sorry."

"It's nothing." She handed Jacqueline a small bottle of water. "Here, drink this. I'm going to run up the hill and collect the group. Stay here and rest a while. I'll be ten minutes. There's a bathroom in the back if you need it."

When the tour guide was gone, the driver hopped up and stood on the first step in the well. He lit a cigarette and, blowing the smoke outside, watched Jacqueline in a way that was familiar and that she did not like.

"Hi," she said.

The man raised his chin, but said nothing in reply. He kept pulling on his cigarette and giving her cold, lingering looks.

She finished her bottle of water, stood up, hoisted her pack onto her shoulders, and prepared to leave, but was struck again by an intense feeling of nausea. The man flicked his cigarette out the door and set his gaze on her. She wanted off the bus, wanted to be free of it, to go vomit in the trees somewhere, in the wind, in peace, but it was rising in her and she could not imagine pushing past him. She could not touch him or breathe his acrid smell. So instead, she turned and walked to the back of the bus. Pushed herself into the toilet, pushed her pack onto the sink, and locked the door. Then she bent over and vomited chocolate and water and acid bile into the bowl.

You see, her mother said, pressing a damp cloth to Jacqueline's forehead, you must not depend on anyone. You must not give anything of yourself to anyone until you are certain. Until you are sure that you are safe. Otherwise, for now, no one. Look at you. Weak. Imprisoned. Indebted. Just like your father, my heart. Just like your father.

She wiped her mouth with a square of toilet paper. Then Jacqueline raised up, closed her eyes, and turned to face the mirror. She took a long breath.

There she was—gaunt, cheeks hollow, eyes flat. It was a shock to see herself, not because she was thin and tired, but because it was strange to be reminded of her own face, strange to connect the person she'd been living with all this time to the face before her. The two seemed entirely separate.

There were four quiet knocks on the door. "Are you in there, Jackie. Jacqueline? Are you okay?"

"Be out in just a second."

"Sure, take your time. But we're going to get going, okay? Have to get these people home."

It seemed inconceivable to her that the bus was now full, all of those people waiting for her. It felt a disaster. She would open that door and be the absolute focus of every one of them.

"No," Jacqueline said. "Just need a minute and I'm off."

"We'll give you a ride down. It's fine. We're stopping in Fira and then Imerovigli and then Oìa. We can take you all the way back to your apartment. Take your time."

Jacqueline was silent. She felt the jolt of the bus slipping into gear. She was already being taken away.

"Okay," she said, pushing her head against the mirror. "I have to meet my husband in Fira anyway," she whispered, but there was no answer.

She washed her face in the sink and did what she could to make herself appear clean. She straightened her back.

"Really?" she whispered. "That's wonderful."

She practiced surprise. She practiced interest. She adjusted her tank top. She smiled at herself. She tried a silent laugh. She looked into her eyes. And then, with what felt like a final breath before plunging deep into water, she unlocked the door. She stepped out into the aisle. She saw the driver's black eyes in the wide rearview mirror.

The hum of conversation vanished as she made her way, row by row, toward the front of the bus.

The tour guide, who had been leaning forward speaking

in Greek to the driver, sat up and turned as if alerted by the lull in conversation. "Come sit here," she said, raising her hand.

Jacqueline saw the woman's smile and the driver's eyes at once.

You must speak. You must fight. You must be resilient and charming.

"Sorry, everyone," Jacqueline said. "Have to learn to eat breakfast."

A heavy woman with a terribly sunburned face turned and gave Jacqueline a friendly look.

Jacqueline rolled her eyes and shook her head to say, Idiot me, silly woman, what can you do? It was her mother's trick, her mother's lie.

Callie moved over to the window and Jacqueline took her place.

"Are you feeling better, *mana mou*?"

"What's that you're saying?"

"Oh, it's like sweetheart, I guess."

"*Mana mou*," Jacqueline repeated.

The road wound down in long snaking turns. The bus groaned in the downshift. She watched the landscape pass and then as the road straightened she could see high above her, the mountaintop and for a flashing moment what she thought were her cypresses. Already she was so far from that bed, that view, that brief home. Again, she was leaving. Again, she was abandoning a place, relinquishing a safe present, for some unsure future.

She strained to see the trees, those familiar rocks, remnants of a garrison, peaceful amphitheater, but the bus had taken a turn. The mountain was behind them and all she could see now were green vineyards descending to the western coast, the sea, and thin dark silhouettes of islands in the far distance. Again, she was tumbling away. Blind and without control.

Forward, her mother said. Forward.

Jacqueline nodded and, for the first time in hours, was capable of taking a full breath.

THE BUS GLIDES along smooth asphalt roads. Telephone poles pop past. Cars whip by. The sky is cloudless. Rows and rows of vines. She's on her bicycle, steering with one hand, running her fingers along a picket and wire fence. The bus turns gently away from the sea. Jacqueline is tired. She's at peace. The soft seat beneath her. She closes her eyes. She takes another long breath. She crosses her arms tight around her pack. Saifa's nails are still wet with red polish. There are cotton balls between her toes. There is a storm building over the ocean. The polish is called Pure Passion. The clouds are so dark. They gather and gather and gather. Rain is already battering the ocean. The two of them are side by side. Four legs, four feet, twenty toes and, beyond, the rain coming. The thunder only a quiet rumbling. They hold hands and prepare to run. Saifa will jump up and move on her heels. They will both laugh when Jacqueline trips over the end of her chair and from behind the screen they'll watch as the lightning cuts and cuts and cuts.

YOU MAY NOT RELAX, her mother said as if she regretted it. You may not sleep here, my heart. You must wake up, you must wake up.

The bus was stopped and idling in front of a small hotel. The doors were open and there were people passing by her

seat. Out the window she could see Callie talking to the sunburned woman.

You will need to decide what is next. You must not wait.

She could smell cigarette smoke and was grateful not
to find the driver's eyes in the mirror. None of the tourists
left on the bus seemed to notice her. She should stand and
walk off the bus here, but she could not get herself to stand.
The prospect of going out into the heat—no, not the heat,
the heat wasn't what kept her there. It was the prospect of
noise that was most daunting. The rush of cars and wind and
voices. She was so grateful for the shelter of that bus. Its
insulation and quiet.

You must make a decision. She'll try to take you to Oìa.
You should get off here. And if not, if you're too weak for that,
then in Fira, but you've already run from Fira. Fira is full of
police.

Yes, Jacqueline thought. But she made no move. And
there was the driver, who looked at her again dead on, and
although she should have turned her eyes away, provided no
challenge, she held his gaze with a fierceness that broke him.
He turned and took his place behind the wheel and with two
hands put on his sunglasses.

If he was watching her in the mirror, he was doing so like
a coward.

I'll get off in Fira, she said to her mother, who nodded
and rolled a lime back and forth over the countertop.

"I'll get off in Fira," she said to the tour guide when she
took her seat. "I have to meet my husband there anyway."

"Sure," the woman said.

The bus stopped in a lot just off of the main square. Jacqueline had not constructed a plan. The doors were open,
people were up and filing out, but she stayed still and kept
her face turned to the window. She was not ready with a
story. She was too tired to move. There were taxis out there.
She watched a group of kids all dressed in matching yellow

T-shirts. There were signs for Internet cafés and beyond them, in the distance, was the road out of town bordered on both sides by tall eucalyptus trees. There was a pair of policemen smoking in front of a news kiosk.

"We're here," the tour guide said.

Jacqueline didn't respond. She kept her face to the window and closed her eyes.

"*Mana mou,*" the tour guide whispered, and then Jacqueline felt the woman's soft fingers on the back of her neck. She shivered and turned.

"Sorry," she said. "Sorry. I was somewhere else."

"You've had a rough day. You sure you don't want us to take you on to Oìa? We're headed there anyway."

"No, thank you. I have to meet my husband."

"Sure," the woman said.

The lie was as obvious as anything.

The two women descended the bus and stood together in the heat.

"Well, thank you," Jacqueline said. "Thank you, Callie."

"It's nothing."

"Well."

"Listen, if you ever need to find me. Here." She held out a card. "In case you lost the first one."

The driver was nowhere.

"Please thank the driver for me," Jacqueline said, gauging the woman's eyes, but they betrayed no plot, no collusion.

She took the card. "In case I do." She reached out and touched the woman's arm. "You've been very kind," she said and walked away.

SHE WENT IN THE DIRECTION of the main square where she'd once been so hungry, where she'd sat on the pharmacy steps. How long ago had that been? Time ran out behind her like blood.

Time runs out before you, my heart. It extends and extends. Into the distance, into the future. You are young. You are a girl. You have lives and lives to live. What's passed will fade.

Jacqueline knew her mother was lying. She crossed the square and stood in line at the gyro shop, where she spent seven euros on two—one lamb, one pork—and a can of Coke.

Reckless, irresponsible child.

She carried her lunch to a shaded bench facing the square and for those next minutes was aware of nothing but that food. And when she'd finished it all, and there was no nausea, when she didn't feel like vomiting, she took a full breath.

Three policemen walked past. Jacqueline crossed one leg over the other and began folding the wax paper into quarters. They paid her no attention and now she thought she'd made the right decision to return here. Stronger now, there was something brave in that. A suggestion of something vital in her, something she'd forgotten. It was a brief rise of confidence, an irrational sense of something she couldn't quite identify. Desire maybe. Aspiration.

Hope, her mother whispered and ran her nails against the back of Jacqueline's neck. She did it like she was pulling her fingers from the keys of a piano, one after the other, pinky to pointer.

But it was not her mother who touched her neck that

way. Those were Bernard's fingers. That was his gesture. It had been misappropriated by time. Or because of it.

He was walking toward her in a loose white cotton shirt. He was looking at her, squinting in his way, an act of estimation, which was, in those late days, his version of a smile. Then she could smell him. Hotel soap and sweat and Speed Stick. She could feel his face rough against her breast, his soft hair beneath her hand, the sound of the air conditioner starting and stopping.

The memory of those late afternoons caused something to fall inside her, and whatever brightness had come from the food, from the rush of sugar and caffeine, was replaced by longing.

They were alone on some dirty Monrovia beach. He was talking and talking and she listened to him the way she always did—enthralled by the flow of words. He talked and talked and she watched the waves rising up out of the ocean and slamming onto the sand. The foam all white in the sun and the sky turning to storm. She loved to listen to him. Not the words themselves, just the sound rolling out and out. She was already convinced by then—about Ghankay, about the absurdity of her job, about all of it. Even about her father, though Bernard never said it exactly. He talked and talked. He was so full of reason and disgust. So full of facts. The truth, he said to her. The truth is, he said. Open your eyes. Look, Jacqueline, look around.

He was twenty-seven when they met. She was eighteen and he'd laughed at her. As if she were a child. I've seen the beaches, yes. Shaking his head. Superior. Yes, I've seen your beautiful beaches. Flirting. And already admonishing her.

He came and went. Filing stories from Sierra Leone, Guinea, Côte d'Ivoire. Gone for months. Once nearly an entire year. But he always came back and always with his disgust, his contempt. So full of things to say. Nearly six years of Bernard coming and going, coming and going. Six years of his talking.

Of his rage. Of his tenderness. Of his promises. Of those dark eyes suddenly before her, suddenly gone.

She'd mistaken his contempt for conviction.

What kind of a man, her mother began.

But Jacqueline stood up. She carried her trash to a can, dropped it, and kept walking. She made her way off the open plaza and into the narrow streets. She climbed upward, not seeing anything. She did not maintain the right expression, she did not walk in the lazy, easy style of the people she passed. She was not demure. She was a central point of energy on every street. Her face was hard, she walked with power and direction and everyone who saw her coming kept their distance.

Be careful, my love. This is how you end up in jail.

But Jacqueline sucked her teeth and dismissed her mother with a furious shake of her head. And soon she arrived at the top of the town. Anyone in her way, she would have knocked over. She dared people to hold her eyes, she dared them all to challenge her. She was ready to fight now. She would have fought anyone who came at her, but no one did.

She split the crowds. There were no police. No one stopped her.

She crossed a path cobbled with fragments of pale limestone and black lava rock. She entered a small green park, and from here, breathing hard, she saw the water far below lying still in the ruined bowl of the caldera like something that wasn't quite water at all, a thing between liquid and solid and of a color unlike any she'd seen. She stood on that sharp edge of cliff, her forearms on a rock wall, and looked down on the small barren island in the middle, which was Nea Kameni. She watched the wind break the stillness and blow rough tracks across the surface of the water.

She was calm. Something pulled at her, it seemed. As if from within, drawing her downward, somewhere solid. So high above all that blue, that treeless island, perhaps it was vertigo. But she did not feel off balance or dizzied. Instead she felt powerful, she felt a moment's peace, released from an otherwise constant rage and anxiety and terror.

And how do you explain that?

Need I?

Of course you do, her mother said. Of course you do. She wore a black A-line dress and was clipping her toenails into an empty bathtub.

Jacqueline watched a massive cruise ship enter the caldera. The water looked so unlike water that Jacqueline imagined the ship to be moving on invisible rails.

Now she was here. All that motion and disaster and chaos. And then: here. Here with her pack at her feet and her stomach full of food and twenty euros in her pocket and a foolish sense of calm.

That is God, my heart.

Twice, her mother said. Don't shake your head. Twice, you've felt it. That weight. That power. That calm. And how many times have you seen it? The good that's come to you. The safety you've enjoyed. You came with nothing, my little girl. Nothing. And now here you are.

I have what I came here with. Plus an idiotic visor, someone's old ChapStick, some money. Sand in a plastic bag.

Her mother smiled at this.

Jacqueline smiled as well—brief and faint.

And life, love. Life.

I came here with life.

Her mother didn't respond.

Now she was here. Once again perched somewhere looking down onto a world below, faced with the same question. Always the same question.

Your life is what is made by the answers to those questions. To all the thousands and thousands of answers to those questions.

Is that true?

Of course, it's true.

Jacqueline wasn't sure. She wasn't sure she understood what her mother meant.

What are your choices now?

Jacqueline didn't respond.

Jacqueline, her mother said. What are your choices now?

"I don't know," she whispered aloud, feeling the calm evaporate. Now she was a homeless woman in a public park whispering to herself.

It was coming undone again.

Answer me.

I can stay at this wall, in this place, or I can leave and go somewhere else.

Yes, her mother said as they walked together through Trafalgar Square.

These were her choices.

She didn't know where else to go.

You could go to Oìa, her mother said. I hear it's lovely and, of course, your husband is waiting for you.

Waiting for me the way *your* husband is waiting, Jacqueline hissed.

The cruise ship inched along, a toy dragged by fishing line across a frozen lake.

If I go to Oìa, there will be another wall and the same choice.

That is called living, my heart, her mother said, kissing Jacqueline's forehead, tucking her into bed. She looked down on her daughter sadly and said again, That is called living.

What was once an island is now the ruins of an island.

She looked at the small cone of Nea Kameni. Like a dormant fountain, she thought.

But it is not dormant. The nice woman told you. It could go anytime. Anytime at all.

A swimming pool rode the back of the cruise ship.

A rectangle the color of sky, so much paler than sea.

Sometimes in the late afternoons they drank Club beer

at his hotel. In the early days, when they'd first met, when that hotel was a place to drink beer and watch the waves through the razor wire. When Jacqueline was there to hustle journalists. Before it became a bunker, a place for stringers and aid workers to hide and pray. Their table was just inside a portico, where the breeze was amplified, and they had a straight view over the pool and out to the ocean.

Jacqueline couldn't remember their conversations. Maybe they hadn't talked at all. Maybe that was the ritual. Just the slow fall into evening. Just the two of them at their table drinking beer from the bottle, while outside the hotel skinny boys sprayed white UN Land Cruisers clean for cash.

The ship below was still as a building.

She remembered their waitress. There had been an unusual softness about her and in those evenings she was a part of their ritual.

But what had Jacqueline said to Bernard? What had he said to her? For a while they'd talked about the country, about the stories he was filing, about his life before her, about her life before him. But all of that seemed so much earlier than those evenings at the hotel.

There was a time when he'd be away a week in the north reporting on the LURD for the AFP and when he came back he'd tell her about Sekou Conneh.

They're not fucking around, Jackie. They've got the whole north. They're coming.

She listened to him and remembered what he said, but only to use against her father in her sad, too-late rebellion. As things got worse out there, as those children in the jungle were developing a taste for cocaine, all she wanted from Bernard were stories of the Blue Lake in Tubmanburg, a place her father talked about as if it were Liberia's own wonder of the world.

"It's a mining pit filled with water, Jackie," Bernard said.

The journalists knew Jacqueline, knew who her father was, and what she wasn't, knew Bernard, of course. Still, there had been a fight once. An aid worker, someone from the UN she thought, had leaned over and whispered a question in Bernard's ear, and Bernard had stood and hit the man in the face with his nearly empty bottle. He'd held it not from the neck, but in his palm like a grenade. The glass didn't break and the man bled over his white shirt. Jacqueline saw it now with such clarity—the blood running down his face and staining that clean white fabric in drops. That she saw as if it were happening now on this wall, as if the shirt were in her fingers, but still she could not remember what they said to each other in those last months.

Perhaps they hadn't spoken at all.

Now she was very tired. She found a low bench and sat with her arms crossed over her breasts. She let the weight of her head draw her chin down so that all she could see were her wrists, her bare arms.

His fingers traced along her skin. His middle finger gliding in curves along the soft inside of her arm from the mole on her bicep to the very center of her palm. She on her back, a white sheet drawn up to her waist. The window open to the ocean. The air heavy and warm. Bernard propped up on his side, his fingers moving over her body. Her eyes closed, a palm now caressing her shoulders, so soft along her face, over her breasts, her stomach, the back of a nail along her hip bone where the skin was thinnest. She remembered his hand returning to her breast, a welcome weight. The television floated there for a moment, until she saw that it was fixed to a rack bolted to the wall. There were oranges arranged in a pyramid on the dresser.

She felt the warmth of his chest against her cheek. The breeze came up and brought the smell of ocean air and wood smoke. In this position, when he was on his back and she on her side, she liked to wrap her leg around his and fix herself to him—a kind of grounding. Her cheek to him, her hand flat, her thumb moving over the rise where his chest ended and the stomach muscles began.

She saw all of this in the sky before her.

She could feel him whispering into her skin, into her hair.

But she couldn't hear him. Either of them in those last months.

She ran her fingers over the soft skin of the inside of her arm.

And then he was gone.

And she was returned to the bench, to her present life, to the endlessness of choice.

To the *facts,* her father said.

And those are these:

You are alone.

You have the clothes you're wearing.

You have the contents of your pack.

Including twenty euros.

It will soon be night.

It will soon be colder.

You are thirsty.

You will soon be hungry again.

II

THE TEMPERATURE WAS FALLING. There were decisions to make, an unrelenting present pressing down on her, and all she wanted then was for Bernard to draw the sheet and the thin cotton blanket over them both, to feel his knees fit behind hers, to feel his chest against her back, to close her eyes against her rotting country, against the coming night, against the rising wind, against this bench, against the inevitable, cold red sunset, against the bus driver's eyes and the guide's oiled legs, against her own blathering mother, against Saifa's eyes, against those ghost boys and their jackal father.

But all the wanting in the world, her mother reminded her, will leave you with exactly what you have.

And it was true. For all that desire, a desire that hung heavy and mean in her gut, she remained where she was: holding herself in her own arms, her skin turned to gooseflesh, while the earth rolled back from the sun with devastating speed.

And it was the speed, if nothing else, that provided some solace. For if it moved like that, it would always move like that, and somehow, because of it, things change, somehow things end.

Look, her mother said. You are not a child. You may not sit here wishing. We don't have time for that kind of self-indulgence. The problems are immediate. Where will you sleep? She looked up from the cutting board and pointed a paring knife at Jacqueline, holding it like an ice pick, not to slice but to puncture. Tonight? Where will you sleep?

It could not be there in the park on that bench. The path was crowded with tourists. So she forced herself up and descended back into the town to find a shop, a place to buy food and water, and then to find a place to sleep.

And that would be all she'd think about.

First the food. Then the bed and nothing more.

Jacqueline walked through the main square and out along the road, where the fragrant eucalyptus trees spread above her against the sky. She walked until she found a small grocery.

She bought two liters of water, hard rolls, a bag of almonds.

Fruit, her mother said, and so she bought tomatoes and peaches.

She reached for a thick bar of milk chocolate.

Reckless girl, her mother said.

And so she bought a block of Kasseri instead. But cheese doesn't last.

It'll last longer than that chocolate will, little pig.

She left the store, and rather than continue along the main road she turned up a side street. The sun was gone from the sky and what was left were the remnant reds dissolving into blue. At this hour the island seemed even further delineated—every surface broken by clean line and sharp shape. The texture was gone as if the physical world before her had been cut from dark and heavy paper.

Soon she came out onto the footpath that ran along the caldera. She was farther along to the north now in the direction of Imerovigli and far beyond, of Òia. Nea Kameni was a shadow on the steel water. Cruise ships were motionless, lit up bright. A small boat moved along the far coast.

Jacqueline followed the path out of town. The dark was descending fast and far ahead of her, lights were coming on, illuminating low white buildings, domed churches, small restaurants. Abruptly, here, the path was no longer illuminated and turned occasionally to dirt, and soon she was nearly invisible. This dark stretch between the two towns was made up of small homes and half-built hotels, an occasional church in disrepair, a few tavernas.

It is simple: you are looking for a place to live. One thing and then the next thing.

Again, Jacqueline wasn't sure who was speaking.

She passed a low building blocked off with a makeshift plywood fence.

She could see the outline of a small cement mixer. A stack of disassembled scaffolding. It was built in the style of all the cinderblock buildings on the island—rounded roof, cavernous, plastered. This one remained gray, waiting to be painted white and trimmed in blue.

She gripped the top of the fence and stared at the little cement mixer. She held her breath and listened, but there was no sound, and when it felt right, she pulled a section of plywood back, slipped through, and returned the wood to where it had been. She crossed the dirt yard and passed through the arched entryway. Inside, she stood quietly in the dark, waiting for her eyes to adjust.

She added *flashlight* to her list.

The dim light from outside cut a long blue triangle across the concrete floor, but the depths of the building remained in blackness. She did not have the courage to push deeper, so she imagined the dark a solid wall and dropped her pack and the plastic bags of food. She sat on the damp floor, beneath a glassless window, and closed her eyes.

She tore a roll open and filled it with a chunk of the white cheese. She used her teeth again to tear pieces out of the tomato.

She ate her dinner and drank water from a bottle and was happy to feel the food change her. Happy for the little warmth, the clarity of mind.

She ate a peach for dessert and then, when she was finished sucking all the fruit from the pit, reached above her and placed it on the window ledge.

At least today she'd eaten well.

Yes, her mother said as the thrill of solving immediate

problems began to dissolve, but you will always need to eat well. You will always need to have shelter and privacy and safety. We are in search of permanence.

Permanence, Jacqueline repeated.

So far as it exists, my heart. Don't fight me. Tonight you sleep. In the morning we will see where we've landed.

Jacqueline spread her blanket across the floor. She removed her sandals and laid her head on the pillow made of sand. She missed her cave and its mattress. She missed the pine needles and her cypress trees.

You see, her mother said, the way it happens? You don't think of your home, your blankets and pillows and sheets drawn tight, drawn smooth. Now you dream of cardboard and garbage. You dream of dead trees. You see? Time is God, my love. Time is God.

She closed her eyes and listened.

A dog barked at slow intervals. Not the rapid, hysterical barks of desperation. The sound was plaintive and certain. After some time, the barking stopped, and so she listened to the wind rushing through the building. With each gust, something rattled in the far dark behind her, behind the imagined wall.

She drew the blanket over her face and tried to make herself still, but with every fade toward sleep, whenever she felt herself being drawn away, her body wouldn't allow it. She shook. Her heart wouldn't rest. She felt her throat constricting. Soon she could no longer keep her eyes closed and now stared into the blanket's dull darkness. It seemed to her that she would have to decide between being suffocated and throwing the blanket from her face, risk exposing herself to the cold air, to whatever it was that waited for her, rattling in the black.

It was the calculus of night. Of sleeplessness. She knew this.

She knew this, but for what felt like a very long time, she could not bring herself to push the blanket away. The air was hot and fetid. She wanted to breathe but still she remained below, beneath, pressed down, her eyelashes catching against the worn fabric.

She thought she might chew through the cotton, cut an air hole, and so brought a bit of blanket down into her mouth, sucked it in, the salt on her tongue, saliva running, she began to gnaw at it, sawing her front teeth sideways. She was seeking air. A way to be protected without being smothered to death. It was the logic of night, of half-sleep, of terror.

Her mother said, Stop it. Her mother said, Take it out of your mouth. Easy now. Easy, she said, and cooled her hands on a sweating glass full of ice and tonic and lime and gin and held her daughter's cheeks. Easy, angel, easy, she said, peeling the blanket from Jacqueline's face, wresting it gently from between her teeth. The blanket for a moment sharp as a dart, its point between Jacqueline's lips, and then going limp and gone. Her mother massaged Jacqueline's jaw where the muscles roped. You were dreaming, her mother said. Just dreaming. Soft hand, cool on her daughter's damp forehead.

But she was not dreaming. Had not been dreaming. Was awake all that time, she knew. Awake when she tried to chew through the blanket like a rat. And the rattling was still there resonating in the darkness. The wind twisted and ran across the caldera, raced up and over the sharp cliff edge and through the spaces in the plywood wall and into this dark and doorless building where Jacqueline lay, no longer suffocating, where at any moment, if she were to make a sound, the mean and dirty edge of a machete would be brought down across her throat. Down against her skull. Lengthwise. Split like a nectarine.

So she did not sleep. She breathed through her nose slow on the seven count, seven in, seven out, until the sun bleached the dark from the room. Then after she turned her head and squinted and saw forming in the depths the empty socket at the end of its wire shuddering against the fresh, gray concrete wall, she turned her back on it and closed her eyes, and breathed and slept until the morning gave way to the afternoon.

And in the afternoon, when the sunlight fell full across her legs and warmed her cold feet, she brought herself up onto her elbows, arched her back, and let her head fall, finding something soothing in the sound of her cracking neck. Still, she was stiff. Her hip bone on the left side was bruised and tender.

She stood up slow and cautious. Like an old woman, she thought. The room had yet to be divided and was just an open rectangle. A cement staircase rose through the ceiling into the next floor. At intervals, there were capped wires bending out of uncovered outlet boxes. A ladder lay atop a pile of folded canvas. There was the light socket of the night before, and all the others along the ceiling hanging down like pruned branches. Like the claws of plastic animals. There was plumbing. Capped pipes in the two back corners. An open drain covered in screen.

She squatted at the back of the room and ran her fingers over the metal outlet box, held the stiff wires in her hand.

Were they coming back? Had the building been abandoned?

This is not the place, her mother said.

Jacqueline climbed the stairs. The domed ceiling arched above her. Plywood blocked out a single window at the front of the room. Sunlight edged around it. She pressed her cheek to the rough wood, and squinted through the light. There was the empty sky, the caldera below it. The path. The entrance to this building, this house.

This is not the place, her mother repeated. That look on her face meaning, I know you before you know yourself. Know what you imagine, know your foolishness. And the answer is, No, the answer is, No, this is not the place.

Jacqueline withdrew from the wood. She imagined the place a fortress. Somewhere from which to defend herself, somewhere to look out onto the world.

She slid her fingers into the light and gripped the wood. She wanted to pull it out, fill the room with air.

No, her mother said.

She wanted a chair, to press her bare feet against the sill. Light on her face.

Leave it where it is. You are trespassing.

She left it where it was and began to walk a slow circle around the room.

She wanted a chair. She sat on the floor and leaned against the back wall. She watched the window until all she saw was the outline of light—like something drawn in neon.

She wanted a chair. She wanted Saifa.

Saifa.

She began to ask the question, but stopped herself. She didn't need her mother to tell her what those questions were worth.

Her mother cleared her throat, but Jacqueline didn't need reminding. She dared her mother to say what she would say: But you cannot understand, but you cannot know, you should not try, but trust, have faith, etcetera, etcetera.

But she was silent. Her mother wasn't in that room.

Nor her father.

Nor Saifa.

Nor Bernard.

No one was in the room but Jacqueline. So she fixed her eyes on that frame of light and tried her best to fill the room anyway.

First, there were Saifa's feet. Calloused. Toenails painted. Pure Passion. She could see the bottle, its cap and tiny brush.

Jacqueline unclenched her fists, opened her hands, and turned them upward. The feet were there, heels in her palms. She wanted to say more, but all she could find was the name.

"Saifa, Saifa, Saifa." On and on and nothing more.

"Saifa." The girl running across the lawn chasing a feral orange cat.

"Saifa." The woman standing at the edge there where the grass broke into jungle, looking down on the shantytown below, belly in her hands as if it weren't a part of her at all.

Looking down on the tarps. Late dusk. Fires burning. Fires flaring yellow and settling to orange.

All quiet, the city besieged by then, the lull, the hollow pressure. No longer possible to lie, to make believe. The pantomime ended.

And yet they were in that house as if nothing but benevolent spirits waited for them out there in the night.

They waited: willful, arrogant, stupid, blind, proud.

As if everything she had hated in their father, everything Saifa had ignored in him, had come all at once to be law. That house, that land, had become its own country. Those last days, their own isolated and stubborn king, housebound, pacing the halls, dressed to rule, dressed to *work*. His ruby tie knotted fat and high, suit jacket fastened by a single button, thick gold-nibbed fountain pen in his fist. His loyal queen, stubborn in her own faith, gliding through the house in her elegant Italian dress the color of a pale and unpolluted sea, in her highest heels, a darker green, drinking gin and tonic and the juice of a whole lime, her glass rattling with ice cubes. Ice cubes because there was no reason *not* to run the generator. Everything would always be easy to come by. There was nothing to protect against. No catastrophe to prepare for. No reason to save gasoline. Run it and keep the house cold, keep the freezer going.

She longed for her family as they were years ago, a particular version, a version that may have never existed. She wanted those three people to occupy the bare concrete room.

She did not want her recent father. She wanted the younger man. She wanted the early history. The man possessed with the stillness of certainty, of happiness. She did not want that pacing and weakened fool, but she could not filter memory.

Despite her father's determined blindness, Jacqueline believed Bernard, who had been telling her for months that it had all ended. Bernard had told her and she believed him.

He would not be surprised if Taylor was already gone. Gone to Libya, or even to America, hidden there by the

CIA, or if nowhere else to Nigeria. Anywhere else but here in this pit. He was willing to bet that he'd already fled. And if he hadn't he would soon. The captain would not drown with the crew, he said, and Jacqueline knew it was true. The country was no longer his. No longer theirs. They were all absurd, Bernard said, dressed up in their houses. He had seen the LURD. Had spoken with them, had been to their camps, seen the men, listened to them calling themselves captain and commander. *They* were dressed for war, and not some cocktail party. He'd seen those children, their eyes. He had seen them rip out a man's intestines and use them for rope. Rope for a checkpoint. Strung across a road, Jacqueline. Time had run out. Like it or not, he said with an arrogance so similar to her father's. An arrogance and even some satisfaction, as if perhaps in hating Taylor, in partly hating her father, he also hated Jacqueline. If only immediately. There at the hotel, out on the terrace in the heavy heat, in those moments as if there were no difference between any of them.

"Idiots on a hill," he said and may as well have spit.

As if she still needed convincing. As if it were so simple to condemn one's father.

"So what next?" she asked.

"*On verra,*" he said. "The first thing is to get out safely when the time comes."

Jacqueline nodded.

"And the time is coming quickly," he said with satisfaction. As if he'd won. Proven his point. Wise and world-weary journalist. He'd seen it all. "And you wanted me to write about the beaches."

She returned her face to the plywood and looked out at the blue day. It was the same. The caldera remained. The water remained. A couple passed. A dog trotted by. Great ships were on the water. Sailboats.

When the wind came up she could feel it cold against her open eye.

Gradually she came to understand that she'd have to continue on. Here she would be found out. She would never feel in possession of this place.

Her mother, of course, was right.

She could not leave in daylight, though. She watched herself, a black woman coming out of a construction site, sliding the plywood back, stepping onto the path. No. She would have to leave at night. Until then, she was a prisoner. Until then, she would have to wait alone with her mind.

When she woke her jaw was sore. She could not remember her dreams. The sun had set and the room was graying quickly into darkness. She folded the blanket and packed her bag. She went upstairs, and in an act of quiet rebellion, she carefully pulled the plywood from the window. If she stood back and kept in the shadows, no one would see her. The path was unlit below. There were more people out now, and from the shadows she watched the couples strolling along, the children running by, all the feral dogs in search of their suppers. The sun had set over the other side of the island and had left the sky above the caldera streaked with blood.

For a while she faded from herself. The wind softened, turned to gentle currents of air.

She was waiting for a lull in the foot traffic. She thought of Bernard. And from there she came to a decision. An absolute decision, a point of certainty that went beyond what was necessary, and in so doing felt buoyant.

She could hear her mother in the distance, in the other room, coming up the stairs, calling from outside, saying, Be careful, my heart, be careful. Think of what you can control, think of what's next, but Jacqueline stepped forward and crossed the line of shadow that fell across the floor. She moved closer to the window so that her whole body was there for anyone to see. She laid her palms flat against the rough sill, kept her arms straight, and leaned forward to feel the air more fully on her face. She gave her arms her weight.

She could see her own silhouette.

She looked up at herself from the street and saw a dark figure, a regal shadow framed in the wide window of an unfinished house. Like a dictator, face obscured, looking down upon a great square.

The decision was simple: Wherever this ends, whenever I stop, whenever I have a kitchen and a bedroom and shelves for my things—that place will be somewhere open, somewhere high, somewhere like this, somewhere like the house in Mamba Point, like the cave, like the cypress tree and the bed of needles. Wherever this ends, she thought, wherever I stop and what's next begins, whenever that is, it must be somewhere far above everything else.

What kind of decision is that? her mother asked. What good does that do?

But Jacqueline didn't listen. She knew she had to leave soon. Still, she waited a bit longer, strengthened by her meaningless decision, by the passing world, by the rising light to the east, the rising light, which might have been a far-off city, but that she knew was the moon.

Now she would have to leave. There was no more time to wait.

The figure vanished into the shadows and was replaced by a rectangle of black.

Jacqueline descended the stairs, picked up her bag, and made her way quickly across the dirt yard, paused at the fence, pulled the wood back, and then she was gone.

———

Now Jacqueline was a woman enjoying the evening.

She followed the path and soon she was walking in the

light of quiet tavernas. Here she drew herself up and prepared to smile.

She did not know what she looked like, so she stopped
and pretended to consider a menu board. Those who noticed
gave her only a glance. The waiter raised his eyebrows and
pointed to an empty seat. She smiled and shook her head. It
was as much a mirror as was necessary.

She continued on. She could hear the hollow, percus-
sive sound of people in a swimming pool behind the walls
of a hotel. There were taxis waiting. Drivers standing in the
streets smoking cigarettes.

And then she was out of town. The moon had come up
behind her. First it was rust-colored. As it rose, it yellowed
and then paled to the whitest blue.

There were no more buildings. The path turned to
crushed lava rock. There was no more wall. The moonlight
cast Jacqueline's shadow before her. She listened to her sandals crunching against the path. As she walked, it was the
only noise she could hear. When she stopped and stayed still,
there was the faintest sound of water sloshing against the
rocks below.

The path dropped away and disappeared into shadow,
then it rose again and followed a steep ridgeline, marked
by occasional white stone cairns reflecting the moonlight.
Beyond the top of the ridge, she could no longer see where
the path went, but she knew that there was that last town.
And even if she'd not thought it precisely, she knew that was
where she was going. As if she'd been heading there all along.
As if from the beginning she'd had that town in mind.

She climbed onto a warm boulder and removed her
sandals.

What beginning? her mother asked without any acid in
her voice. She asked it calmly, as if she were interested and
had no lesson to provide. She asked as if with hope. That
perhaps her daughter had come to understand something
important.

Jacqueline didn't know what beginning she meant, but she felt it anyway. No matter how momentary this fit of certainty. It would pass. It might pass halfway up the ridge, or before she could slide her feet back into her sandals, but now, she was calmed by it. Foolish and illogical and dangerous, she was calmed by it.

She waited a while longer, drank some water, and then tried to remain as still as possible. It was not only the rock that held the heat, but the valley itself; its black walls radiated warmth between themselves. And Jacqueline in the middle. She imagined them speaking to one another—the walls, the water, the moon, her mother, herself. She could not imagine what any of them were saying, but she imagined them speaking nonetheless. She felt joyous and clear and she worried again that she might be going mad, that this was the start of lunacy.

Then she saw herself back on that beach. She was unwashed and laughing to herself, the Senegalese men mocking her, tossing her scraps of meat. She saw herself wearing a pair of cheap sunglasses for their amusement. On her knees, the neck of a wooden giraffe between her teeth.

She closed her eyes and stood naked beneath the shower, under the orange light. She climbed into her cave. She was clean and dry and warm beneath her blanket, and from here she could look out onto the bay and watch the lights of the boats pass silently in the night like satellites.

When she opened her eyes she understood, again, that the battle was the same.

She would have to climb the ridge and continue on in the direction of the last town. It was there she'd been heading all along.

And her mother said nothing. Only bowed her head and smiled.

And Jacqueline, not quite ready to continue, waited a little longer, listening to the wordless language of the valley.

Eventually she stood, raised her arms, and stretched. She

turned away from the water. A dog, thin and wolflike and as white as the cairns, was watching her from the path.

At first, Jacqueline was afraid. The dog was close, maybe twenty-five feet away. But then it dropped its head once in a quick nod. As if it were bowing to her. Jacqueline smiled at this. "Hello."

The sound of her voice was surprising and seemed loud and foreign as if it had come from somewhere other than her own body.

"Hello," she said again to the dog, who bowed again.

Jacqueline laughed and in response the dog sat as if it had been given a command.

She slipped her feet into her sandals, climbed down from the rock, and faced the dog. She extended her hand and again it dropped its head. She approached, carefully closing the distance between them. She kept her hand out and when she was within a few inches of touching the animal's nose, she squatted and said again, "Hello."

She could feel its breath on her hand now. Jacqueline waited until the dog, losing patience for all that formality, stood up, moved forward, and nuzzled her wrist. She stroked its head and scratched its ears. The dog wagged its tail and pushed forward and turned so that it was pressed close to her body.

Jacqueline laughed again and with both hands rubbed its neck and belly while the dog turned tight circles in the small space between them.

The dog was young, she could see now. She ran her hands over its ribs. It was lean and undernourished like all the dogs wandering the island.

"What's your name?" Jacqueline asked. "What's your name?"

The dog licked her chin and rolled onto its back. She rubbed its chest.

"So you're a boy," she said. "What's your name, boy?"

The dog said nothing.

"Well," she said, "it's time we go, don't you think?"

Jacqueline stood. The dog scrambled to his feet.

"Ready?" She asked. They looked at each other, the dog dropped his head, and the two of them descended into the darkness.

Soon they'd reached the very bottom of the valley, so low they could no longer see the moon. Instead of following the path she focused on the dog and like this they made their way.

They moved between giant boulders, sharp hunks of lava rock, gray silhouettes against the blue night sky, through the shadows, protected by the valley walls. She had given herself over to the trail, and to the guidance of the dog trotting expertly forward.

Her mother said nothing, of course. Did not admonish Jacqueline for *this* kind of indulgence. It was *not* the same as spending money on the wrong food. Or becoming too comfortable in a dangerous place. This was something else. This was in a different realm. The realm of spirits and signs. The realm of God.

A white dog does not appear in the night, out of nowhere, for no reason.

Her mother's silence was an argument itself.

This was how to proceed, her mother would say. With faith.

Jacqueline was irritated by her mother's arrogance, her condescension, but she was in no mood for a fight. So she did her best to ignore the serene and knowing look. That familiar expression: I am certain. And you are a fool.

She wanted not to think. She wanted to follow. She wanted to move through the night and consider nothing but the moonlight and what to name the dog. She did not want to argue, but it was too late. She could feel the rise of anger.

Saifa was at the edge of the lawn looking out over the ocean. Saifa cradling her belly in her hands, the orange cat working figure eights through her long skirt, between her solid legs. The boys were coming up the hill. Jacqueline knew this before the boys themselves.

The argument was so old. It was exhausted. Wrung out. Leave it be, she told herself, and yet it continued to cause her such rage. Her mother a victim of her own stupidity, her own blindness. She hated her for it, even in death she hated her for it. Hated all of them. Above all, her father.

And yet, sometimes, there were moments. Moments when it was undeniable.

It?

Something. Call it what you will. At certain times of day. In certain places, in certain wind. Beneath the moon. Under the protection of a warm valley. Under the protection of a white dog who appears out of nowhere. A skinny white dog who drops his head the way this one does. Who, rather than staying at your heels, leads you instead. Who looks back from time to time to make sure you're following.

So the rage was twofold: that kind of stupidity, stupidity you call faith, the stupidity that killed us. And yet it exists in me as well and you are responsible for that too.

You who in the end I discovered to be arrogant, proud, lazy, drunk, and broken.

They began to climb. Jacqueline walked hard. Furious. Ahead was the sharp line between shadow and moonlight. She watched the dog cross it, watched him turn back and look for her. She wondered if down here she was invisible to him. The path grew steeper. She had to shift her weight forward to keep her balance. Once she crossed out of the dark, she stopped to rest. The dog was waiting for her.

She could see the caldera again, could see back to the other side of the valley, could barely make out the path she'd descended, could see the lights of Fira, and far to the south the lights of smaller towns. And somewhere out there, beyond what she could see, was the black sand beach, and her cave and her cardboard bed, and the man who'd given her lunch.

And beyond that.

They pushed forward. She continued to follow the dog. As they climbed the gradually rising ridgeline, the valley no longer protected them from the wind.

Jacqueline watched. Woman and dog silhouetted against the sky. Just the two of them marching forward, as if there were some warm bed waiting for her. As if she were coming home to someone, as if Bernard had prepared a meal for her on his hotel hot plate, as if there were bowls of food and water waiting for the dog. As if there were a door to close and bolt behind them.

They walked on and on, the woman and the dog, as if they were expected.

Far ahead, at the very top of this last rise, Jacqueline could see an unlit building pressed against the sky.

Soon they arrived at a small church. They came up from behind it and then made their way around to the main door, where a cement terrace was fronted by a low plaster wall. The dog had leaped up and was now standing and panting and looking out over the island's last town. Jacqueline stood next to him for a moment, and then sat with her legs hanging over the edge. Below, the path dropped away steeply at first and then rolled out gradually.

Here was Oìa.

The lights began near the base of the small mountain, where they were only intermittently scattered. Then they began to gather in a concentrated light. At the far end of the town, they narrowed so as to form the shape of a bird— a fat egret maybe—with its head at Jacqueline's feet, then the long neck, then the bright body, and its tail hanging above the water, where the lights ended.

Among it all were shapes of translucent green and blue. Lit swimming pools, which looked to Jacqueline exactly like the glass beads she once kept beneath her bed in a yellow metal Twinings tea box.

She imagined it was the view that caused the dog to be so suddenly still. She reached for him and stroked the soft fur at the back of his neck.

Jacqueline knew that to go down into it, this last town, was the inevitable thing. She had reached the end and whatever was to happen would happen here. There was no logic to this, and yet she knew that it was true. It was possible to turn around, but she knew she would not. She'd come for this beautiful town, with its lights, its glass beads. She knew this and yet she also knew that she would wait. That she would stay above it for the night, maybe several nights. First, something needed to be prepared. She wasn't sure what that was, or what she meant, but she knew it nonetheless.

So she opened her pack and removed the bread and cheese and a tomato. She spread these things out and pretended to ignore the dog, who sniffed and nudged her arm with his snout. And then as she tore the last roll in half and laid a slab of cheese across it and tore pieces of the tomato with her teeth and dropped those across the cheese, the dog licked her cheek. Jacqueline added almonds, closed the sandwich, and tried to avoid the dog, who was licking her neck. She held the sandwich tight together to seal it, pressing the tomato into the stale bread, and now she laughed and said aloud, "Hey, hey, stop it," and pushed him away with her shoulder.

The dog moved his eyes between Jacqueline's and the sandwich. She smiled at him and in return he dropped his head twice as if to say, Hurry up. Ignoring her mother, she fed him a piece. Then she ate. Each time she looked over at the dog something shifted in her chest and she knew that she would feed him the last bit. And after he'd finished it she gave him her hands to lick clean.

She found the water bottle, which was less than half full, and drank. She poured a bit into her palm and watched him lap it up.

The bread was gone. There was a tomato. A few almonds. A peach. A bit of cheese. Again, she would have to buy food.

The dog was curled up at her side. Jacqueline was trying to count the glass beads. She followed one to another. It seemed as if someone had thrown them over the town and they'd rolled and gotten stuck between the white buildings, caught at the cliff edge.

The church door was chained and padlocked, so she crossed the path and began to climb.

The hilltop was wide and fell away gently in all directions. As she walked she watched the dog dodging through the moonlight. There were no trees. Only scrub brush and boulders. Some of them big enough to cast wide shadows across the ground. It was behind one of those massive boulders that Jacqueline dropped her bag. She watched the dog mark their night's territory. She swept the area of rocks, spread her blanket over the ground, arranged the pillow beneath her head, and watched the sky. She lay in the shadow of the rock while all around her the moon cast the world in silver and blue. She turned her head and watched the wind blow through a thyme bush.

She called for the dog. "Hey," she said. She whistled her father's whistle. Quick breath in, quick breath out. High note, low note. High note, low note, but the dog didn't come. She extended her arm and watched her hand cross out of the shadow and turn to silver. She snapped her fingers. "Hey," she called again. "Come here, boy."

She returned her hand beneath the blanket.

She would have liked him to sleep at her side, to feel his warm body against hers.

She dreamed of the orange cat turning its figure eights around Saifa's legs and Saifa, her back to the house, her hands on her belly, standing motionless looking out over the ocean. The cat was bright as flame and its fur seemed to be the only source of light in the yard. It paced and paced through the long skirts, which rose and fell over the cat's body like gauze.

When Jacqueline woke, she was sweating. The moon had set, and in the darkness she wished for her sister. She wished for her mother. And then, in spite of herself, she wished for Bernard. For the sound of his voice. But all she could hear aside from the wind moving through the thyme bushes was her father sobbing as they brought him into the kitchen. This was what her memory gave in return for wishing.

She wished the dog would return.

She wished this island would erupt again and turn her to ash.

She wished she could hold Saifa's feet in her hands.

Instead her father was led gently into the kitchen, his hands bound behind his back. Her father in his fine navy suit pushed to his knees to join his wife—each of them with their hands bound, her mother silent, her father sobbing and sobbing.

And where were you?

Now her mother spoke.

Where were you? My proud and principled girl.

You know, Jacqueline said.

Yes. Yes, I do know.

To fight it, Jacqueline thought of the letters she'd sent Bernard at the beginning. She thought of her box of red envelopes and their razor edges. She tried to imagine what she'd written to him, the kinds of things she might have said.

She wished for those letters.

She wanted to read them, to see the kind of person she'd been. Not even a year, but she could barely remember. She wished she'd kept copies. Records of herself as something other than what she was now.

You are what you always were, her mother said, her voice now gentle. My girl with the enormous heart. My brave and stubborn girl. You are what you always were. You must remember that.

But Jacqueline knew this was not true. She was no longer whatever she'd been. Still, she'd like to see those letters. They were the only record and she'd like to see them. They'd be evidence of something.

Dear Bernard, I am sitting here, outside the house, looking at the ocean. The storm has cleared and the sun will set soon. Now all I need is you. Just you. I want nothing else. Do you understand that? I don't want anything more than you and to be somewhere like this. Somewhere with a table and a bed and view over the world.

Who had she been to write like that? Capable of such silly romance. Paying some kid to run her envelopes to the hotel.

She imagined he'd kept them, that somewhere in a drawer in Nice were all of those letters in a neat bundle wrapped with rough twine the way they are in movies. She imagined that he was there waiting for her. That he was out there somewhere searching for her. None of this was true, she knew. She'd never called him. He'd done as much as he would do.

Jacqueline was falling to sleep.

She could see him searching for her. She could see him searching for the woman who had written all those letters, the woman who had folded them and sealed them in red envelopes and had them delivered not even a mile from her house, to the front desk of the Mamba Point Hotel, where someone would walk to his room and slip them beneath the door.

III

WHEN JACQUELINE WOKE, it was light out and the sun was just beginning to rise. She was cold and very tired and her back was sore. She walked a few feet away to pee. Her legs hurt. Her feet hurt. Everything seemed to have been taken from her in the night. It was all she could do to stand and draw her underwear back up.

She folded her blanket. She finished what was left of the water. There would be no more waiting.

No wallowing, her mother said.

Jacqueline sat on the rock and faced the sun. She ate the last peach. The warmth, the sweetness and acid of the fruit brought her some energy. She did not look at the town below, but she knew that today she would descend the path.

It was inevitable, this descent, this entry. In one way or another, something would end here.

She flung the pit away, opened her eyes, and stood up on the rock. She turned her back to the sun, her shadow stretching long in front of her. There were the patchwork farms and vineyards sloping gently to the white frothing coastline. There was the church, pink as bloodied water, and beyond that the cliff edge and the caldera below. She looked down over the town, the buildings like white teeth piled at the very edge of the cliff, at the very end of the island. White teeth and beads of glass.

Only go down the path. Only find water. Find food. Find shelter.

She climbed off the rock and changed into her last pair of clean underwear, her last clean tank top. With her mouth, she wetted the thumb and forefinger of her right hand, and used them to clean the sleep from her eyes. She removed the visor from the pack, brushed the dirt off, and tightened the Velcro band around her head. She tried to see herself. She changed expressions. She smiled. She raised her eyebrows in surprise. She played with spoken language.

"Nice to meet you," she said. "Hello. How are you? Where are you from? What do you do? What is your name? What is your name? What is your name?"

The words seemed to echo and rattle in her head long after the wind disintegrated them.

She walked down the trail with Saifa at her side. She was atop her father's shoulders, her fingers on his forehead. She held her mother's hand.

She was alone. There was nothing of them left. Nothing but memory and memory seemed like madness. As the path took her farther down, as she listened to her mind, and the wind, and the sound of her footsteps, she was again having a difficult time distinguishing between madness and memory.

She walked on and on down the hill. The path steepened and turned and all she wanted then was to walk with someone else, to not to have to enter this town alone, and the feeling took her over, became dread, became terror. She wanted to stop walking, but she knew that walking was the only thing she could do. Stopping might kill her.

Like a little shark, her mother said.

She continued to walk until the path flattened out and the town became individual buildings, small hotels with swimming pools, and then it rose up and became the parking lot of a desalination plant, and then picked up again and became a wide paved walkway from which narrow paths descended past low wooden gates, down the cliff edge to individual hotels, and houses with tiny swimming pools and terraces painted the color of storm clouds and trimmed with white. She continued walking along the main path and soon there were people. Early-morning walkers, and hotel employees in white shirts and name tags. Her heart had slowed, but still, as she made her way along the pathway, past all the whitewashed buildings, she wished and wished that she were not alone.

Now as the path ended, she stopped walking. She stood in front of a small market, which faced the main road. Across the street was a taverna.

The market was closed. She sat on a bench outside and rested. From time to time a delivery truck passed, the occasional taxi. Otherwise, it was quiet. It would be nice, she thought, to sit somewhere and eat breakfast.

What she wanted above all was a cup of coffee. Very hot with cream and sugar. She could feel the smooth cup in her hands. And like that, she had direction. This was the advantage of desire. Desire focused the mind. It eliminated extraneous thought. The greater the desire, the less the burden of the mind. She would like to live her life this way. Perhaps it was how to survive intact. Live to satisfy her desires. Desire only what she could have.

That cup of coffee possessed her. It was all she wanted. For the moment, there was nothing else.

She crossed the street. She could just see over a long white wall onto a broad terrace where there were set tables. The entrance to the restaurant was an arched arbor covered with pink bougainvillea. From here she could see past the tables and into the building. The doors were open.

She took a breath and crossed the terrace. She found a table. It felt good to sit in a chair. It felt good to run her palms over the clean white paper tablecloth. Overhead, more bougainvillea trained through a wooden trellis, which filtered the sun and dappled her table with rounded squares of pale light. She could feel those squares warm against her bare neck.

She checked the zippered compartment. A single bill. Twenty euros. A few coins.

All that's left, her father said.

All that's left, she agreed.

We must always take stock, he said. Be clear with yourself. Know what's there and what isn't. Don't imagine. What you see is what you have. Nothing more. No fantasy will change that, do you understand?

Hypocrite.

Jacqueline wanted a cup of coffee.

She sat up straight and pressed her palms against the paper and waited. She was the only one on the terrace and wasn't sure if anyone had noticed her or even if the restaurant was open. She watched the building and began to think about going inside. She would have to stand and cross all that space. It was not something she wanted to do, but she was prepared for it. She would do it like any tourist impatient for service, impatient for her morning coffee.

But then came a young woman dressed in jeans and a white T-shirt, her hair pulled back in a loose ponytail. When she was close enough, Jacqueline could see that she had a pretty face. Round and soft with narrow eyes and a wide mouth. She came to the table and spoke in Greek. And then in English, "Good morning."

"Good morning," Jacqueline said in return.

"Some breakfast?" The woman covered her mouth with the back of her hand and yawned.

"Coffee, please. Very strong coffee."

"Nothing else?"

"Not for now. Thank you."

The woman returned to the kitchen.

Jacqueline was buoyed by the exchange. There was something in its normalcy, its familiarity. She liked the way the woman had yawned, the ease with which she had smiled.

Jacqueline moved her left hand back and forth over the paper, watching her fingers crossing through the sunlight.

The woman returned with a pot of coffee, a cup, a spoon, and two small pitchers on a tray. She put everything on the table.

"Coffee," she said.

"Thank you."

"Nothing else?"

"Not for now."

The woman slipped a laminated menu between the sugar and saltshaker.

When Jacqueline was alone she tore two sugar packets open and emptied them into the bottom of her cup. She added cream and then poured the coffee. She stirred it all together with the spoon, wrapped her cool, dry hands around the cup, and raised it to her lips.

And there it was. The thing she wanted. Coffee with cream and sugar. Everything was right. The flavor of the coffee, the heat, the fat, the sugar. She finished and made another; this time she let the liquid stay longer in her mouth, trying to taste it.

By the time she'd finished the second cup she could feel the heat inside her, the caffeine moving in her blood. Her vision became clear. It was as if she'd barely been alive. She wanted to talk. She was ready to go on. She felt such a rush of confidence she had to stop herself from laughing aloud. She poured another and leaned back in her chair.

She saw all the pink flowers above her, the shards of blue sky beyond them.

Maybe she *would* order something to eat. She glanced at the menu and considered picking it up. But if she did that, it would be impossible to control herself. In her bag there were some almonds, the remnants of the cheese. One way or another she would need more food.

I am taking stock, you see?

Her father was looking at her from across their little table at Astoria Restaurant on Carey Street. Long before Bernard. Before the LURD meant anything to her, before she'd ever heard the name. Before Saifa had reached puberty. Jacqueline and her father. Every Saturday afternoon. Just the two of them eating lunch together. The waitresses rushing to wipe the sticky wooden tables clean whenever they came in the door. Whatever else he had, he always ordered groundnut soup.

Over those lunches, when sometimes he allowed her two or even three Cokes, they would talk and talk. They'd come in and she'd wait while he moved through the room smiling and kissing cheeks and shaking hands. When he was finished, he'd put his arm around her shoulders and they'd take their table opposite the front door, and here he would turn all of his attention to Jacqueline. For those hours he would barely look away from her. She looked forward to those lunches all week. She wouldn't have given them up for anything in her life.

JaJa, how is school? Tell me about school. Tell me about these boys your mother says are chasing you. Should I have them shot? I will have them shot tomorrow. Tell me the one you like the most and I'll have him shot first. Or maybe we'll cut his head off. Chop off his hands. Give him some long sleeves.

No one was funnier than he. No one more brilliant. No one more handsome. She laughed until she couldn't breathe. She threw bread at him and told him to stop. And each Saturday, she relished the moments when she'd look away for a moment and notice people watching and she was reminded of the way they were, how uncommon it was. She could see them in the eyes of others. Saw jealousy and joy and wonder. It was the pleasure of belonging to a private and impenetrable club. She was just then beginning to play at being something other than a girl. During those lunches she experimented with posture, upright with her hands on her lap or slumped back in contrived ease. Both feet on the floor. Or legs crossed. And when her father said that she was beautiful—Oh, JaJa, as beautiful as the sea—then she believed that it was true.

And what will you do with your life, my beautiful daughter?

How old was she then? When had that tradition begun? How old had she been? Ten? Eleven? The years before they'd sent her to England.

My lovely daughter. Young woman, what will you do with

your life? It is not too early, you know. It's not too early to answer those questions.

She shrugged.

It is not up to the universe to decide. And the sooner you know, the sooner you can begin. You are not one to wait around for inspiration like your mother. Signs from God. You are different than she is. *We* are different than she is.

Jacqueline nodded.

Don't wait, JaJa. Don't wait, her father said.

Her father who died of waiting.

Be practical, he said. Take stock of your life.

To tell a little girl to take stock of her life! Her mother shook her head. They were walking somewhere. Jacqueline could see her mother's bare feet. Ignore that foolish man. Go to school. Stay out of trouble. Be a child while you still can. Life will take that away from you soon enough.

Jacqueline nodded, but her loyalty had been won. She said nothing, but her faith was with her father. And no eleven-year-old girl wants to remain a child. She wants to sit in a restaurant across from a handsome man who never looks away from her, who smiles as if she is the source of all his joy.

What will you become? her father asked. A young woman like you, beautiful as the sea, must take stock of her life.

"I would like scrambled eggs and toast," Jacqueline said. She hadn't even picked up the menu, but when the waitress returned and asked again about breakfast, she'd said scrambled eggs and toast. To hell with it, she thought.

The waitress repeated the order, "Scrambled eggs and toast. More coffee?"

"Yes, please," Jacqueline said. "And some water too."

The woman turned to go, but Jacqueline stopped her.

"Wait," she said. "I'm sorry, but the coffee, is it free? I mean the second pot."

"Oh. Yes. Okay," the woman said as if they'd come to an agreement. "Okay, yes, the coffee is free. The second time."

"Okay," Jacqueline said, embarrassed. "Thank you."

"Do not worry."

"It's always better to know," Jacqueline said, mimicking her father.

The woman nodded and returned to the kitchen.

While she waited, Jacqueline tried not to worry. She tried only to wait. She tried to wait without memory. She tried to wait with the light on her table and the upright menu and the salt and the pepper and the ceramic rectangle that held the sugar packets. She wondered what that rectangle was called. A sugar packet holder? She wondered where they were made and how one buys a sugar packet holder. She tried to lose herself in this wondering, but it was no good.

Her father smiled at her from across the table.

She and her mother held hands as they walked along the white beach.

Saifa jumped up and down at the edge of the lagoon.

The wind blew an umbrella end over end across the sand.

Jacqueline took a sugar packet between her fingers and shook its contents down.

The skirts moved like gauze over the back of the orange cat. Saifa held her belly like an object separate from herself. She began to turn to the right. Inch by inch until her shoulder pointed at the house. The orange cat ran its figure eights between Saifa's legs. Its fur was as bright as fire. There was noise below. Laughter. The boys were calling from down the hill.

My beautiful girl, her father said. My daughter. His eyes were bright and young. He was handsome and proud. He touched the knot of his tie.

Look at that girl, her mother said, pointing down the beach, where Saifa, four, five years old, was holding hands with a thin boy in flame-orange trunks too big for his tiny waist.

Jacqueline looked.

Look at her, she said and laughed as Saifa threw her arms

around the boy's neck and toppled them both into the shallow water.

Jacqueline watched the waitress walk out of the restaurant carrying a wooden tray across the terrace.

"Breakfast," she said, arranging the food on the table.

A white plate piled with scrambled eggs. A basket of toast wrapped in blue cloth. Pats of butter wrapped in gold foil. A small bowl of strawberry jam. Fork and knife and spoon rolled in a paper napkin. A glass. A tall bottle of water.

The waitress arranged these things with delicate care—each object delivered with grace. As if she could feel Jacqueline's hunger, as if she sensed that this meal was somehow sacred. Jacqueline waited with her hands in her lap, her head slightly bowed, and felt the woman moving around her. She watched the empty coffee pot rise up off the table. She watched another land softly in its place.

"Coffee. The second time free," the waitress said.

Jacqueline turned her head and glanced up. Their eyes met and the woman smiled.

"*Bon appétit.*"

"Thank you," Jacqueline said and smiled back.

When the waitress had gone, she began.

She unwrapped two pats of butter and with the knife scraped them onto the eggs. She added black pepper. She reached into the warm basket, removed a triangle of toast, and buttered it. She added sugar and cream to her cup and poured the hot coffee.

She laid the napkin across her lap.

She put a forkful of the eggs onto the toast and then Jacqueline began to eat.

The immediate pleasure. The feeling of warm food in her mouth, the flavor of the eggs, the overwhelming taste of salt, the faint burn of pepper.

Everything else had been annihilated. A euphoric obliteration of memory.

There was only the eating, which she did as slowly as

she could—portioning out the eggs and toast, allowing one extra triangle, which, when the eggs were gone, she buttered and topped with jam. When all of it was gone, she drank cup after cup of the hot, sweet coffee, and when that was gone she leaned away from the table and began to drink the cold water.

She was not ready to stop eating even if her stomach already hurt. She ran her finger across the plate collecting egg yolk and butter and bread crumbs and sucked her finger clean. She bit down lightly on the knife and drew it out of her mouth to collect the remaining jam.

Already she could feel herself returning. Or memory returning to her. Or her mind. Or whatever it was that came rushing back. Call it memory, she thought. And for a time the act of eating displaced memory. It was like a solid thing in a pool of water and the second you removed it, the water returned. It was always like this. And she began to understand that to live, one must be able to live with memory because memory was the constant. Even for her, even in such a pre-carious life, when there was danger and uncertainty every-where, when her immediate life demanded so much of her, still, memory was the constant.

Jacqueline was barely conscious of the waitress, who had returned to clear away the plates, who may have said some-thing to her, asked her some question.

She felt the water rushing back to replace the solid ob-ject. It was the slow fading away of ecstasy.

Now she saw the pyramid of oranges on the dresser. The open window. The smell of sex giving way to the smell of the ocean, to everything else that was outside. One thing fading, another thing taking its place. Orgasm giving way to sadness. Joy giving way to gloom.

Bernard just returned, or about to leave, and Jacqueline always in one place, day after day wishing he'd come back, or wishing he wouldn't go. And all those days so convinced of some kind of permanence, terrified that this would be her whole dull life—the car to work, the phone calls, the same drinks, the same conversations with the same journalists, the car home, the long, dull nights with her family. Dinners and listening to the radio and her parents arguing or laughing and Saifa doing her homework, feet on Jacqueline's lap, and all the while Jacqueline wished for him, for the hum of his endless monologues, his hands, and then the quiet of their room.

She could feel his hand moving from her breast, over her stomach, a solid pressure. This she loved above all—when it was over, once they'd caught their breath, his cool hand fit tightly between her legs, his thick palm pressing as if to soothe her. She thought of it as a kind of bridge between one world and another. She loved to lie in his arms like that. Bernard propped up on his elbow, the sheet drawn to their waists, her eyes closed. She fell asleep that way. Fell through the sadness of another afternoon ended. Fell through the sadness of that inevitable return, and into sleep. Sleep, the last separation, and then in the early evening she would wake and waking was worst of all.

Jacqueline looked up from the table. There was the bottle of water and her glass. The wind was rising. The squares of light flashed on the table as the flowers moved above her. Her stomach cramped. She stood up, took her bag, and walked as slowly as she could manage toward the restaurant. Inside, it was dark. There were a few tables and at one of them a man with smoothed-back silver hair sat smoking while he entered numbers into an adding machine, the tape unfurling around a yellow mug.

"Bathroom?" She'd been more abrupt than usual. She'd not included her solicitous smile, not demurred, not bowed her head or fluttered her lashes.

Without looking up the man gestured with his head away from the kitchen. She found the bathroom down the short hallway, pulled the door closed, locked it, and sat. She bent over in pain, sick with diarrhea. She began to sweat. She waited for her body.

At least, she thought, I am here instead of somewhere else. At least there is this toilet. At least the door locks. At least there is paper.

She waited while everything went out of her. She was consumed by the pain. It stabbed at her. And then, when that subsided, it was dull and round. She stayed bent over, sweating, enduring it, wishing it away.

Again, as with eating, there was nothing else and when, eventually, it was over, she thought, Pain too is a solid thing. Pain too displaces memory.

Now, standing at the sink, she was exhausted. She ran warm water over her hands and scrubbed them together, the pink liquid soap turning to lather. She removed her visor and rested it on the toilet tank. She dampened a brown paper towel with hot water and wiped away the cool sweat on the back of her neck, on her forehead. She pressed the hot paper to her closed eyes, to her dry lips.

And then, finally, she looked at the mirror. She was not so bad off, she thought. Thinner, certainly. Her cheekbones even more pronounced. Her eyes a little hollow perhaps. But all in all she was not the horror she'd begun to imagine. Her hair was a bit longer, which softened her angular face. Her skin was smooth and not entirely dull. Perhaps that was the water, but it didn't matter. In this mirror anyway, it appeared she was still alive.

She moved the ChapStick over her lips, leaving a cool burn where the skin had cracked. She wished she had some lotion for her face. Perfume. But she stopped herself before the wishing went on.

She dried her hands, then ran a finger over the ChapStick and used it around her eyes, over her cheeks. She washed her armpits, left them damp, and opened the door.

On the terrace she could feel the air moving around her eyes, her lips, her cheeks—the menthol sharpening sensation.

The waitress had customers, and from her table, Jacqueline watched her work. Soon the woman came over and put her hand on Jacqueline's shoulder.

"You are okay?"

The gesture was a surprise.

"Yes, yes," she said. "I'm fine."

"You were gone for long. I thought maybe you were sick."

"No, no," Jacqueline said. "I'm fine. I'm sorry to take so long."

"Good then," the woman said, removing her hand. "I'm glad. Okay. You'd like anything else?"

"No, thank you. Just the bill."

The waitress nodded and placed it facedown on the table.

"Take your time," she said.

It was five for the eggs, two for the toast, two for the water, and there was one fifty more for something else she couldn't make out. The coffee, she figured. Eleven euros. More than half of what was left. She was a fool.

She found the twenty and laid it on the table between the bill and the saltshaker.

Soon the waitress came back.

"Okay?" she asked.

"Okay," Jacqueline said. "This, the one fifty, it's for the coffee?"

"No, no. That is the cover. Always a cover in Greece to sit down."

"Oh, I didn't know."

"Many people don't know in the beginning," the woman said.

"And the coffee?"

"Today the coffee is free. Both."

Jacqueline looked up and saw the woman's eyes. "Thank you," she said.

"Nothing," the woman said as she looked away and began to make change. She laid the five on the table and the two coins on top.

"Thank you," Jacqueline said. "It was very good."

The woman touched her shoulder again. "Have a good day."

Jacqueline watched her walk away. Younger than I am, she thought.

More charity. What was it the woman saw in her face that Jacqueline herself couldn't see in the bathroom? She needed to identify that element so that she could remove it. Unless, of course, the element was simply her color. No mystery at all. Was being black on this island equivalent to being some kind of refugee? In Spain, she had seen both.

On the beach in Valencia, she'd watched a tall woman, Sudanese she'd guessed, approach two black American women who were drunk and laughing beneath a broad blue umbrella. When the woman approached with a board of beaded necklaces, the two of them sobered and waved her away.

She'd thought then, Well, I can be one or I can be the other here. But perhaps the same wasn't true on this little island. She saw the blanket and its neat rows of sunglasses. She saw the Senegalese man waiting for her at the top of the stairs. Felt his fingernails tearing across her arm.

She thought of the drunken Spanish man who'd crossed the wide beach in Málaga. Who'd crossed all that sand only to spit on her and kick her in the ribs and scream and scream in his slurred and incomprehensible language. She'd been sitting alone on the sand looking out at the sea, her blanket around her shoulders, and he'd come storming silently from the promenade across the beach expressly to kick her.

So, if there were something in her face, some mysterious element she could not yet see, she'd have to find and remove it. But if it was simply her skin, then that was another problem and one to be ignored.

And now, with her stomach still cramping, she capped the water bottle and stood up from the table. She was surprised to find the terrace filled with people. She saw now that the restaurant was attached to a hotel, a narrow white building trimmed with blue.

She waited for the waitress and when she came out, a plate of food in each hand, Jacqueline waved. The woman raised one of the plates in farewell.

———————

SHE CAME TO THE BEGINNING of a worn white marble pedestrian street. It was early still, but there were a few tourists out strolling in the morning sunshine. Jacqueline tried to emulate their casual gait. They were unlike the frantic tourists in Fira who came off the cruise ships with only a few hours to spend their money.

She passed art galleries and restaurants, jewelry stores and cafés, bars and hotels. All of them were quiet, all of them small. There were other, narrower streets that broke off this one, and down them to the left she could see flashes of blue water. She was transfixed by the town. Its polished paths and low buildings, and all its lovely order. She continued on until she came to a wide square, in front of the main church. She sat at one of the benches at the perimeter of the square and watched two men talking and spinning worry beads. Neither seemed to notice her. One of them pushed a hand through his gray hair and spoke. The other laughed and began to cough. Then they both returned to their original postures—upright and the beads spinning around and back, around and back.

Jacqueline waited.

She needed to find a place to sleep.

What had changed? What would change? She could hear her parents, but somehow their voices were farther away. What was left to say? She'd started to bore them.

To all of it, the same response. Yes, yes, yes, she thought. I know.

A boy in a bright green T-shirt dribbled a rubber soccer ball in a diagonal across the square.

Jacqueline thought of the waitress. That was all. The woman raising the plate of food to say good-bye.

The men spun their worry beads.

She wondered if she might be like them, if she could spend the rest of her life sitting on this bench watching the days change. The shifting light, the rising and falling wind. Whatever else happened here on this square. She imagined the church doors opening and closing to various services. Funerals. Easter. Weddings. Christmas. She looked up at the unlit streetlamps and imagined the square full of people. She would like to be one of them. A woman on a bench. A woman to greet in the mornings. A nod of the head. A wave in the evenings. She would go to a café and they would give her strong, sweet coffee and milk in a cup and serve it to her on a saucer with a spoon, and they would let her take it to the square because she was honorable and would always return it.

She might carry her own worry beads to spin over her own right hand. She might kick the ball back to the children. She might impress them with her skill. Once, with her heel, she could flip a soccer ball from behind, over her head, and have it land in front her. Once, she could juggle it from foot to foot. She was sure she could do those things again. The kids might come to love her. They might know her name and she might know theirs. Some of the bolder young men might flirt with her in the evening wind, beneath the yellow lamplight. One might take her to dinner. Not the most handsome in the square. Someone else, someone calm, someone with tired eyes whose hands were always still. He might come to her, and with one hand push his hair from his forehead. They might drink a bottle of wine together on the terrace of

one of these restaurants. He might put his arm around her
shoulder as they walked along these smooth marble streets.
She might become friends with his mother and sometimes
just the two of them might sneak away from the men and sit
outside somewhere hidden, where they'd get drunk together
and share a cigarette.

Or perhaps, she thought, I'll just be here alone. The
strange black woman with the worry beads. The woman who
stayed while all the other tourists went home. Who refused to
leave even after the weather turned bad, the strange woman
who stayed, who's here every night at her bench. That would
be all right too. Just to be the woman on the square. The
woman who feeds the feral dogs. Who can do that trick with
the soccer ball. That would be okay too, she thought. As long
as they'd let me bring a cup of coffee into the square, let me
sit here with it balancing on a saucer.

Jacqueline took a breath and stood up. She smiled at the
men as she left the square, but they didn't seem to notice.

She wandered on along the walkway, going deeper into
the village until she saw a blue domed church. She turned
down a side street, descended some steps, and stood before
it for a while. She waited here watching tourists take photographs of the dome against the sea.

She thought of going in to find her mother in the cool
half-light, but the door was locked, so she continued on to
the very far end of the island, where she discovered an old
fort, most of it in ruins. She followed some tourists up the
steps. She looked off the edge into the unprotected water
outside the caldera and beyond that where there were other
islands, one fading into another. They were shadows that
went on and on and on.

It was as if the entire earth were made up of these shadow
islands, as if she might step from one to the other for what
remained of her life.

She leaned over the walls to look past the white buildings

clinging to the cliff and down into the water. On the caldera side she could see a long series of wide steps descending steeply to a small protected bay far below.

Then she knew that she would descend those steps, that soon she would no longer be where she was, that next she would be at the water. She'd begun to understand that this was the way her life was made. She moved from one place to another place. Perhaps this is what her mother meant by God, these sudden certainties. God, she thought, always present in retrospect.

As she began to come down from the fort and seek out the wide steps she'd seen, she wondered if she'd already given up her own will. If these instinctual acts were some-how different from will, from decision making.

It did feel to her then that she was being led, as if she had very little to do with where her body went.

You are following beauty, her mother said.

This is the beginning of madness, Jacqueline thought yet again. And then, It cannot always be the beginning of mad-ness. Eventually it has to *be* madness. And perhaps you *are* mad. Perhaps you've *become* mad.

That's the element. That's what they see. That's why they give you food. That's why they pat you. And that's what you cannot see in your own eyes. If you could see it yourself, it would be the beginning. But because you can't, it is now the middle.

———

Now she found herself descending those steep steps with the village to her back and the water below going greener and greener. She could see the tops of colored awnings stretching out from the restaurants below. Brightly painted fishing boats floating anchored in the still bay grew larger as she walked.

The steps were so steep that there were sections where she had to lean back to avoid tumbling forward.

This feeling of being led worried her not only because she knew that nothing led her, but also because she was seduced by the idea. She could feel herself giving in to it, succumbing to the idiotic notion.

Jacqueline had to stop walking and stand off to the side as a train of donkeys passed. On the back of each animal was a nervous and smiling tourist. At the very end, a short man with a dark weathered face followed behind. With a short stick he whipped at the flanks of the last donkey, muttering at the animal as he walked.

When they'd passed, she continued until she reached the bay and its small concrete harbor. Through the radiating heat, she could see a thin man standing shirtless, working a wide grill. He morphed and buckled in the refracting light. Then she was past him, the harbor ended, and she was onto a dirt path. Still she could smell the burning charcoal and the searing octopus.

She came around a gentle turn and here was a rocky beach in a small cove and above it, huge boulders piled high. Instead of settling on the sand, she climbed.

Why? her mother asked, painting her fingernails red with expert strokes of the brush.

Jacqueline ignored the question.

Because they are beautiful, my heart.

And it was true, Jacqueline thought. That was precisely why she'd climbed them. Precisely why she rested here and not below on the sand. She pressed her sore feet to the warm dark stone. That is why she'd traveled a little farther, risked a little more. For no other reason than that the boulders were beautiful.

Her mother said nothing, only smiled to herself.

Jacqueline closed her eyes. And again, she waited.

As the day grew hotter, people began to come around the curve and settle on the sand. Young boys in brightly colored shorts went by as they climbed higher.

The first one frightened her as he plummeted past in a blur of yellow, crashing through the green surface of the water. Then one after the other they sailed by, only a few feet away from her, falling like parrots shot out of the sky—yellow, green, green, red, blue, orange, red, blue—each one rushing so close she could hear their solid bodies displacing air.

Down on the small beach, three pale girls were stretched out in their bikinis. A squat man with a mustache smoothed lotion onto the shoulders of a bare-breasted woman, and beyond them, in the water, a couple swam with their four children.

Jacqueline also wanted to swim. And as the day got hotter and hotter and the small beach became crowded, and the rocks around her began to fill with people, the more she wanted to join them. It felt somehow as if this was as close to the human world as she'd come for a very long time.

She'd been here, and then they'd come.

Those who passed on the way to find their own rocks were quiet and polite, like the boys had been. Some smiled and nodded or said hello in one language or another. The boys were now leaping in swan dives and backflips from the edge of the chapel that had been cut into the smooth southern face of the little rock island across from her. She felt that she was participating in something. As if they were all of them—swimmers and sunbathers, divers and climbers—part of a single thing, a single moment. Buoyed by this feeling, Jacqueline slipped off her long skirt, removed her tank top. She wore the black underwear and bra. Even if it had been the white, she would have gone. There was a man on the rock above her.

"Excuse me," she said.

The man looked up from his book.

"Would you mind watching my things?"

"Okay," he said and smiled. "No problem."

Jacqueline smiled back. "Thank you."

They were neighbors, she thought. Neighbors taking care of each other.

Everything she owned was in that pack.

Your passport, her mother said. The only thing left, my love.

Jacqueline stood up.

When that is gone . . . , her mother began.

But Jacqueline walked to the edge of the rock.

Her mother shook her head and returned to her magazine.

And now Jacqueline was there, standing upright in her underwear.

She let her arms hang to her sides. She could feel people watching. She could feel the wind on her skin. She could see the green water below. How long had it been since she'd bathed? How long since she'd been in the sea? She was euphoric. She dove and saw herself as a blur of black sailing past herself, and then she was in the water and it felt then as if nothing could be the same.

She swam and swam and swam and it was a joy that surpassed the eating. A joy that might have surpassed everything.

She dove down deep and expelled all her breath in a scream.

She came out of the water at the beach and stepped between the bodies to get back to the rocks. She climbed up to hers and there was her pack, and above it, the man.

"Thank you," she said.

He waved it away. "Nothing."

She slept through the afternoon.

It was the absent sun that woke her. She was dry, her skin drawn tight from the salt. She sat up and dressed. It felt as if months had gone by. This was nowhere to sleep. Not on the rock, not on the beach. She would need to find someplace more sheltered, less public, and without too much consideration, without any discussion, she said good-bye to the man, who was no longer there, and clambered down to the beach feeling agile and strong. She passed a group of women and wished them a good evening. They wished her the same.

———————

SHE WALKED AND WALKED. She found a dirt road and followed it where it split from the asphalt. It began to descend and then around a turn she could see the water again, and perched well above, a decrepit building that looked like it might one day become a hotel, or had been once.

The dirt road flowed out into a parking lot. From here a single path ran down through a narrow valley to a beach below. The building extended perpendicular to the track.

There was still a bit of sun left, and she could see two towels down below on the beach—one red, the other white—laid neatly side by side. And in the water beyond, there were two floating figures.

There were no doors on the building. It was just the concrete frame, unfinished like the last place.

"Hello," she called.

But there was no answer. She ducked inside and wandered the structure. There was one large open space in the middle, a lobby, she thought, and then a hallway that ran in both directions.

She stood at all the windows and in the end chose the room farthest from the road. She would sleep here.

Sleep? her mother asked.

Live, Jacqueline said.

Be honest about your plans, her father said.

Jacqueline nodded.

There are few greater crimes than the crime of self-deception.

She listened.

You must always tell yourself the truth. Do you understand me?

She nodded.

Your beliefs must not be beliefs because they are beneficial to you. Do you understand?

She looked up at him.

He stood from the table and brushed his suit clean of imaginary crumbs.

The sun was so low now that Jacqueline could no longer see their colors, but she could see that the swimmers were out of the water and were wrapping themselves in the towels.

It was true. She wasn't thinking only of spending the night in this place. She was thinking she might stay. No nightclubs, no bars. No main road. A reason to be there during the day. Alone and safe at night. Not far from town. Yes, she was thinking, she'd live here. For a while anyway.

You see? her mother said. Things are easy for you. Always a place to stay. Always a way to eat. What do you have to complain about? Nothing.

Keeping an eye on the beach, she unpacked her bag and laid everything out on the floor in front of her. She arranged the blanket in a corner and put the pillow at one end. Here was her bed.

In another corner she arranged her toothbrush, her toothpaste, her napkins, her toilet paper, and her ChapStick. Here was her bathroom.

Along the wall, which faced the large front window, she arranged her clothes and underwear. She collected her passport, and the scraps of paper and cards she kept inside it, and her money and returned them to the zippered compartment of her pack.

There were things to do now. She'd need to build a mat-tress of some kind, find stones for shelves. And there were things to do after that, of course. But for now—for now this one thing was done.

She stood at her window and watched as the swimmers began to walk up the path. She looked forward to greeting them. Hello, she'd like to say. Beautiful evening. How was the water? But as they drew closer, she knew that she could not greet them. She'd have to hide and be silent.

She walked to the room closest to the path, where she sat on the floor beneath the front window. And here she listened as the sound of their voices, and then their footsteps, slipped into the building.

Jacqueline closed her eyes. They were laughing and speaking a language she didn't understand. The noise rose and rose and when they passed, it was as if for a moment they were there in the room with her.

She imagined they were coming to visit. That they'd all sit in chairs on the terrace. Jacqueline would have a hot shower and her skin would be warm from the sun as it was now. She'd wear her white sundress, which she could see hanging from a green plastic hanger in a closet that might no longer exist. They'd sit outside and drink together. Something stron-ger than wine and the three of them would look out over the darkening sea.

She could see the red-threaded hem move, could see it turn to liquid in the breeze.

Fabric moved over fur. Saifa turned toward her. And then there, finally, was her face, eyes flat, and somewhere beyond, somewhere below, were the sounds of yelling and laughter.

Jacqueline walked onto the terrace. The people were gone. The islands were sharp silhouettes. The horizon was burning.

She was alone in her new home and night was coming.

She'd thought she would find her way into town that eve-ning, but she no longer had the strength for it. Instead, she sat on the terrace in the dark and ate the rest of the cheese and the almonds. She drank nearly all the water and then, after peeing at the side of the building, she wrapped herself in the blanket and lay on her back.

The night was windless, the building made no noise, so she heard nothing but the sounds of her body. She had been waiting for sleep to come, but what came in the end was anger, so she began to walk barefoot down the path. The valley was dark, but far out on the water was a brushstroke of moonlight and all the silhouetted islands were hulking unlit ships.

She felt Bernard's warm back against her bare chest.

Soon she could hear the small waves falling onto the sand and then dragging back. The sound grew louder and louder and then she was down with the beach beneath her feet and the foam flaring white, and she was close enough to hear the rocks being pulled by the water, which crashed and rose to encircle her ankles.

She walked the beach now. When she came to one end she stopped for a while to hurl stone after stone as far out as she could, and then she walked in the other direction.

She found a long smooth piece of driftwood and carried it to the other end like a staff.

Then it was a club.

Then a machete.

And then a rifle, which she leveled at the moon.

The sand ended and jagged hunks of lava rock rose up to begin the headland. Beyond was the gentle bay, and its harbor and all the glassy-eyed tourists drinking wine.

She stopped here and standing in shadow, hidden from the moonlight, she was very still. Still, but the anger pulsed in her, vibrated throughout her body. She could feel its clarity, could feel herself alert with it. She waited, and then she could no longer contain it, could no longer be still, and with all her fury turned and swung her stick.

She beat the rock with a wild violence. The first blows hurt her hands, but soon she was numb to that pain. She swung and swung and with each strike let out a quiet groan. She kept her eyes open and swung hard. She swung hard enough to break Bernard's teeth, to shatter his jaw, to crack his skull, to break his fine nose. She swung until he was senseless and bloodied on the beach. She swung hard enough to crush the windpipe of the bearded man. Hard enough to render every one of his dead-eyed boys sterile, hard enough to leave them all in a bloody pile, half-alive, moaning in pain.

She swung and swung and swung until the stick broke in half and she stumbled and fell to the sand, where she lay panting. She could feel the damp rocks hard beneath her and where there was no clothing, points of cold against her bare skin. Her calves, her heels, the backs of her arms, her hands, and more than anywhere, like cubes of ice, the back of her neck.

She closed her eyes and doused the house with the gasoline reserved for the generator and watched the kitchen and that pile of men burning in a brilliant, smokeless fire.

She watched from below, from between the blue tarps, the open sewers, the clapboard shacks of the filthy beach at West Point, as high above it all burned and burned and burned.

————

IN THE MORNING she woke rested and sore. Her hands hurt, her back was stiff, her right hip was bruised from the concrete floor, and there was a long gash across the back of her left hand. Still, she'd slept deeply and had no recollection of ever waking in the night, nor of any of her dreams.

For a moment she could not remember where she was, and for that moment she took pleasure in not knowing, floating there in half-sleep, absent from the earth. She tried not to find the ground, she tried to put off the imminent conclusion, but quickly and again, her mind betrayed her and she remembered.

Jacqueline stayed crouched low as she looked out the windows. She saw no one, but there were two scooters—one red, the other blue—side by side in the parking lot. It frightened her to have slept through the noise of their arrival.

She considered packing the bag, leaving no evidence, but the prospect of once again erasing herself from a place exhausted her. So she left her blanket folded neatly on the floor, left her toiletries where they were, her clothes where they were, and with a breath stood up and walked onto the terrace with her pack slung casually over her shoulder.

Down on the beach there were four people arranging towels beneath an umbrella. Otherwise, she saw no one. She walked up the dirt road until it came to the asphalt. She continued on to the lower end of the village where there was a small bus station. Here, the shops were less elegant, the buildings a bit rougher. Tour buses had begun to arrive. Jacqueline stopped to catch her breath on a bench in the shade of an olive tree. She watched as people climbed down out of the buses and stood in the sunshine, trying to get their bearings.

She picked at the bloodied cut on the back of her hand.

Nostalgia, her father said, is from the Greek. *Nostos,* to return home. *Algos,* pain.

Nostalgia, her father had once told her at lunch, is homesickness.

She crossed the parking lot and walked up a side street past gyro shops, past T-shirts hanging from wooden rods, past cheap jewelry hooked to boards covered in velvet, and soon she was up on the main walkway and in the middle of the village, where everything was polished and clean, where sound was dampened by the vast caldera.

She imagined that everyone here was humbled by its

mass, its beauty, its obvious magic, and so spoke in whispers. Perhaps it wasn't so, but it was certain that the sound was different. And the streets. And the buildings. Everything was kept cleaner, whiter, more humble, as if in deference to beauty.

Or it is out of fear, she thought as she walked along the marble street.

Fear that again they will be destroyed. That they will all be blasted away by the volcano, or that another earthquake will send them tumbling down the cliffs, all those white teeth falling to the water, all those glass beads destroyed, drained of their color.

At the square, the church doors were closed. Two boys were kicking a ball back and forth.

And maybe that was the way to live. Always in fear of ruin.

Beauty as a form of respect. Of superstition.

You see? her mother said.

Perhaps, Jacqueline said. Her father's word. *Perhaps*.

That is it exactly, my heart. Live in fear of God.

Ruin, I said. I didn't mention God.

But they both knew what she meant and so neither of them spoke.

Jacqueline came to the end of the village, stepped off of the marble street, continued along the asphalt road, and soon she was standing in front of the market looking across at the arbor of bougainvillea. Yesterday, she'd not noticed the name, but now she saw the small blue windmill, and the sign—ANEMOMILOS.

She crossed the road, stepped onto the terrace, and took the same seat at the same table. Then the waitress was coming out of the building, a plate of food in each hand, and when she saw Jacqueline she nodded. Once the plates had been delivered to a somber couple with matching sunburns, she came over.

"*Kalimera*," she said.

Jacqueline smiled and repeated the word.

"Good morning," the woman said. "*Kalimera* is good morning."

"I like it," Jacqueline said. "Prettier than good morning."

The woman laughed. "Yes, I think I agree with you."

Jacqueline wanted to know the woman's name. She wanted to say, My name is Jacqueline, and extend her hand.

"So, you've returned. Here again. Coffee and eggs and toast?"

Jacqueline laughed. "Just coffee today, please."

"Nothing to eat?"

"No, thank you. Not today," Jacqueline said, though she was very hungry.

"Coffee," the woman said. "I'm right back."

She rehearsed her introduction—My name is Jacqueline, or, By the way, my name is Jacqueline, or, What's your name, by the way, or, her father's line, Forgive me for asking, but I'd like very much to know your name. Her father, always formal, always overly polite and infuriatingly grammatical, was never more so than when speaking to women.

Forgive me, he said with those dangerous eyes upturned, his fingers moving over some object on the table. Around the rim of a glass, over the tines of a fork, collecting grains of salt on his nail. Forgive me for asking, but I'd like very much to know your name.

Her mother rolled her eyes and looked across the room, pressing her lips together tight.

Your father, she said coldly, is too many things at once. That's a mistake you should never make, JaJa. I forgive myself for being fooled, she said. But a man who can do too much can play too many parts and in the end too many of those parts will have nothing to do with you.

Jacqueline nodded, though she only vaguely understood and at the time there was no man alive more attractive than her father.

A MARKER TO MEASURE DRIFT

Find a simple man, her mother said. Find a man who wants very few things and make certain that most of those things exist.

He wants things that don't exist? Jacqueline asked.

Yes, her mother said. Yes. And that was the end of the discussion.

Later, Jacqueline wondered if she too wanted things that didn't exist.

"Coffee," the waitress said and delivered the pot, the cup on its saucer, the spoon, the pitcher of cream.

"Thank you," she said.

"You will tell me if you decide to eat."

She nodded.

"Good," the woman said and touched Jacqueline's shoulder before returning to the restaurant.

She prepared the cup with cream and sugar and took her time. When the coffee was gone, she went to the bathroom. She peed and washed her hands and face. She applied the ChapStick to her lips. Using her finger, she ran it over her cheeks and beneath her eyes. When she was finished, she wiped a paper towel around the sink and then she returned to her table. She asked the woman for the bill and when it had come, and she had paid for the coffee, and the woman had told her she wouldn't charge her a cover for just a coffee, Jacqueline waved and left.

Tomorrow, she thought, or the next day, she would introduce herself.

I like her, her mother said as Jacqueline waited for a bus to pass.

I know, Jacqueline said.

Your father wouldn't like her.

No?

She's too tough.

No, you're probably right, Jacqueline said. You're probably right.

She crossed the road and went into the small market,

where she spent the rest of her money. She bought a fresh bottle of water and a bag of almonds and the smallest bottle of olive oil they sold. She bought two peaches and a plastic container of cherry tomatoes, which the short man at the register told her he had grown himself.

Now there was no more money. She sat outside on the bench in front of the market and carefully arranged her purchases in the bottom of her pack. She kept one of the peaches in her hand, and when everything was neatly away, she closed her eyes for a moment. When she opened them, the waitress across the street was watching Jacqueline through the arbor.

JACQUELINE ATE THE PEACH as she returned to town.

Where the road broke away, and the marble walkway began, there were now two policemen.

She could feel the rise of adrenaline. So familiar, the dry throat, damp palms, clear vision, thumping heart. She pretended to be occupied by the remnants of the fruit and continued walking.

She could feel them watching. She had seen herself in the mirror. There was nothing to draw their attention. Not that she could see, but what if they saw what was imperceptible to her.

As she approached, she took a deep breath through her nose and raised her eyes to the two men.

She gave them her brightest smile. Eyes wide open, brows arched, all teeth. She would not be the hangdog refugee. She would not lower her head.

The smile seemed to surprise the men.

One of them straightened. The other nodded. "*Kalimera,*" he said.

"Kalimera," Jacqueline responded without hesitating. She put hard emphasis on the third syllable, perhaps too loudly cutting the word apart. She thought the second man, the one who'd greeted her, might have nearly smiled as she passed.

She stepped onto the white marble, the peach pit in her fist, its point cutting into her skin, heart beating hard, and the small of her back damp with sweat.

She moved through the village, waiting for the adrenaline to subside, for her heart to slow. She knew that soon she'd have to sit down, that in a few minutes she'd be so weak she wouldn't be able to stand, that she'd go light-headed. They were always the same, these moments of danger and fear. Or they were the same to her body.

She came to the square, where she found a bench and sat. She looked down at her hand. There was a point of blood at the center of her palm.

She let the pit fall to the ground.

She closed her eyes.

She stood outside the Land Cruiser on the red dirt road surrounded by those boys who stank of cologne. And though she'd never seen them applying it, she could see them now, standing around in the jungle, or in some roadside camp, passing the bottle around, smacking the liquid against their necks, believing their commanders, their lords, that it would make them invincible, superhuman, immortal.

She'd never seen any man use cologne. Not her father, not Bernard, not anyone she'd ever known. But she saw these boys in their camps, passing a squat green bottle from hand to hand, slapping themselves with it, cold and clear.

None of them spoke until they'd crossed the border and were miles into Sierra Leone. Not Jacqueline, not Bernard, not the driver. Were there others in the car? She could no longer remember. She could see the back of the driver's head and Bernard's knees next to hers and the deep, green jungle racing past. Maybe they didn't speak until Freetown. Maybe not until the airport.

No driver. No guard. She had walked vacant through the streets. Anything could have happened to her, but nothing did. Nothing more. She'd come to the hotel, to Bernard's room. Stood in the doorway. No silly seductive lean, no bare foot pressed against the frame.

He gave her the wrong expression. He put her in the car. She heard the door close and then nothing. He was packed. He was leaving. He'd been waiting for his ride out. She could see him looking up at her. He'd have left without her, but there she was at his door. And what could he do? Her escape would be his last burden before ridding himself of her vile country. Of her.

She saw the flash of river and then they were at the Lungi airport, at a café table. There were her hands, flat on the peeling Formica.

She could see him writing telephone numbers across the back of a white card. They'd both looked at the Spanish visa smoothed into her passport. He'd done this for her somehow. She hadn't asked. Some friend. Some phone call. She must have thanked him. Had they spoken then? She could taste the weak tea, could see the cream powder she'd poured into it, the empty sugar packets in a pile, three deep, but she could not hear Bernard's voice.

She left first. He'd held her elbow as if she were an old woman. He'd held her elbow and guided her gently through the sweltering airport as if she'd been someone's grandmother. She hadn't resisted. She'd let him do it. And she'd let him put her on the plane. He'd been patient the way you are when patience won't be needed much longer.

Patient the way you are when you know a thing has ended.

Patient the way you are with those about to die.

She glanced back once. They looked at each other before she went through the door, and then she turned away.

And then there was no more of Bernard.

She remembered the plan, but not the sound of it. Call when you get settled, he would have said. Call from the hotel, call and we'll take it from there. But she couldn't remember him speaking. Not a word. Not a sound.

———————

SHE OPENED HER EYES. Two girls sat across the square. They were leaning in and whispering, holding hands. Sixteen, Jacqueline thought. Saifa's age. She watched them for a while, and then when she'd regained her strength, when her heart had calmed, after she'd scraped the blood from her palm with a fingernail, she stood and continued on.

Instead of walking out to the fort, or down the steep steps to the water, she explored the streets in the direction of the bus station. Here, not all the buildings were polished and clean. There were no restaurants, no bars, no shops, no hotels. This was where people lived.

She turned onto a shaded stone street and walked past the small houses. There was the chatter of televisions, loud voices, none of the reverent hush of the caldera side. Many of the houses were partially whitewashed, and some not at all. She passed small gardens. Staked tomato plants. Lettuce in rows. Not all the lots were inhabited and as she walked she occasionally passed fenced-off properties where only concrete foundations stood.

It was behind the chain-link fence of one of those lots that Jacqueline heard the symphonic mewing of kittens.

Here she stopped, grasped the fence, and looked through the wire diamonds.

She could see the kittens in the sunlight, a nest of them tiny and writhing in the dirt. Their matted fur was brown and white with shocks of yellow.

Jacqueline stared at them through the fence, listening.

She couldn't stay there. Someone would see her.

Through the window of the house next door, she could hear the thin clatter of dishes being washed.

She stayed where she was and watched the kittens.

Thank God, Saifa isn't here, her mother said.

Yes. Jacqueline nodded. Thank God.

She'd be over the fence in a second. Her mother was at the counter cutting oranges for juice. Jacqueline could hear the slice and thunk of the knife blade.

There'd be nothing we could do, her mother said, smiling.

The knife hit the plastic cutting board and the shining orange halves fell away from the blade.

No, probably not.

In the kitchen her mother was on her knees.

In the kitchen her father was on his knees.

Their hands were bound behind their backs.

"Cry," the bearded man said to her father. "Cry."

And her father cried.

Jacqueline could hear the relentless mewing and through the window what sounded like clean dishes being stacked.

Your sister would have saved them, her mother said. But you, you will save yourself.

Jacqueline walked away from the fence and through the little streets until she found the bus station full of arriving tourists.

She left along the hot asphalt street and when she came to it, turned down the dirt road. Soon she could see the hotel and the parking lot, which was full of scooters and cars. She walked onto the terrace and paused. She saw all the colored towels on the beach, a few umbrellas, driven deep into the rough sand.

She snuck inside the room to make sure her things were still there and to leave the food she'd bought and then she descended the path. On the way down, she rebuilt herself, and by the time she heard the water clawing at the rocks, she was ready to return to work.

AND WHEN HAD THAT BEEN ANYWAY? Those days of walking the burning black beach and sleeping in the cave and showering beneath the streetlight. She had no sense of it. How long ago or how long she'd spent there. It made no difference. The facts were the facts.

The facts remain, her father said.

Jacqueline nodded.

You have what you have. You are where you are.

Yes, Jacqueline said.

You have lost what you have lost. You have built what you have built.

SHE DISCOVERED A MAKESHIFT SHOWER at one end of the beach. A hose fixed with a spray nozzle and fastened to a wooden post. She watched a fat man in black trunks place his small laughing son naked beneath it. He counted down while the boy danced his little legs, shivering in place, in anticipation. Jacqueline didn't recognize the numbers, but the cadence was the same. Five, four, three, two, and at one, the man turned on the water. The boy screamed and laughed and tried to run away, but the man scooped him up and the two of them spun beneath the spray.

She kicked off her sandals and put them in her pack and began to walk.

She was looking for groups of women first. She had her bottle of oil.

"Excuse me, do you speak English? I'm sorry to bother you."

She kneeled at the feet of two young girls.

"Two euros for five minutes," she answered.

She'd forgotten her rates. She couldn't remember what they'd been all that time ago. Anyway, better to start cheap.

The one who'd said yes, the heavy one with the long brown hair, fell back onto her white towel like she'd been shot.

Before she crushed it between her hands, the olive oil was a green coin glowing in Jacqueline's palm.

"Oh," the girl said when Jacqueline pressed her thumbs into the muscle. "Oh," she said again, closing her eyes.

She worked the beach for six euros. She might have made more, but she was cautious. Better to be cautious. It should look like fun. Like something on the side. Not a living.

But she was making a living. She played with the expression. It didn't make sense to her. Not literally. To make a living. But that's what she was doing. She was down on the beach making her living. And six euros was enough. She didn't need more than that. Not for now. Not until she had a reason to save. It was enough to eat. It was more than enough. And she should be cautious. She must never appear desperate. It was all for fun. She was a tourist. A student.

When she was finished, she slipped off her skirt and tank top and left them on her pack behind a rock and swam out into the sea, where she floated on her back. She looked up at the sky and when she stopped moving, she felt the salt stinging the wound on the back of her hand.

The stinging is good, her mother said. The salt will prevent infection.

Yes, Jacqueline said. You've told me. I know.

You know everything, my heart. You know all there is to know in the world now.

Jacqueline closed her eyes and sank beneath the surface.
Expelling all the air in her lungs, she fell and fell and fell.

———————

NOW SHE STOOD BENEATH THE SHOWER. The water was
very cold, but she loved the feeling of it cutting away the
dried sweat, the salt, some of the grime.

Afterward, she lay on the warm stones at the back of
the beach.

She thought, I need to buy soap.

Once she was dry, she moved into the shade, where she
stayed until there were only a few people left. When the sun
was low, she returned up the path, past the hotel, and on into
town, where she bought a gyro.

She made her way through the narrow streets and came
up to where the views began, and where the views began the
restaurants and bars began. The sun would set soon. The
tourists were streaming in from the center of the village and
up from the bus station. They were all over the walls, and on
the restaurant terraces, and on the balconies of their hotel
rooms and at the fort they were everywhere. At the ramparts,
and on the stone steps. And every single one of them was facing the sun. Every face lit up the color of new rust. Jacqueline made her way through the crowd and moved carefully
up the steps of the fort. She walked out to the ramparts and
climbed over the wall between two couples. She scrambled
down onto the rocks extending high above the sea and she
sat with the light of the sun full on her face.

From here she saw the cliffs and all the white buildings, and all the people drenched in orange sunlight. She

watched the hushed crowd for a moment and then returned to the falling sun, and the phantom shadow islands beneath it. She unwrapped her sandwich, took a breath, and began to eat.

This is where I have stopped, she thought.

This is where I am now.

This is where I live.

Her mother carried a tall glass across the lawn in this same light. Same color. Same quality.

Her father home from work, still in his suit, sat with his feet extended before him on one of the lounge chairs, the tips of his thick fingers grazing the concrete deck, watching his wife glide through the evening air.

Jacqueline finished her dinner.

When the very top edge of the sun dropped away into the water, the audience applauded. Jacqueline looked back. Three men, all in white, standing on a far wall raised their glasses. Someone whistled in celebration.

The sky above the far islands turned pink and purple and red.

Everyone was leaving down the various meandering streets, or settling in at the restaurants, or returning to their hotel rooms. She walked through town and stopped in a small market, where she spent a euro on a thick bar of white soap.

She passed terraces where people drank and talked.

One night, she thought, I'd like to do that. I'd like to sit and have a glass of wine and watch the sun set, or look out over the caldera.

She continued on through the streets past the tour buses, which were leaving en masse back to Fira. The show was over.

She walked home to her frame of a hotel. All the cars and all the scooters were gone from the parking lot.

The sky over the water was a faded pink and high above it, that strange and luminous blue.

Her things were as she had left them. She undressed and

wrapped herself in her blanket and closed her eyes. She was so tired. She'd forgotten about the mattress again. Tomorrow.

She saw the waitress. She saw her eyes.

She ran her fingers over the wound on the back of her hand.

She pressed for the pain, and then she was asleep.

———————

MORNING AFTER MORNING, when Jacqueline was sure there was no one, that she would not be seen, she stood and stretched and dressed and made her bed.

She'd been lucky and had found, in the trash behind an art gallery, bags of pink packing foam. She'd built her mattress around those bags, two long pieces of cardboard, bound together with rope she made by rolling plastic bags. She tied the whole thing together tight and fit it along the wall. It was a comfortable bed, but on restless nights, the bits of Styrofoam rubbing together drove her mad with their screeching. Still, now she never woke bruised, and the precision of her knots, the geometry of the mattress, the way its corner fit snugly into a corner of the room, pleased her. As did the stone shelves she'd arranged, particularly the flat, oblong rock she used as a bedside table.

Here she kept her squat little flashlight, lens down, and a branch of lemon thyme and a plastic cup, which she filled with water before she went to sleep.

Propped in the far corner there was a long stick, a piece of driftwood she'd brought up from the beach. The nubs of two broken branches functioned as hooks, one for her pack, the other for her visor, whose blue lettering had begun to fade from blue to a green like weathered copper.

There was now a piece of plywood covering most of the front window, which she'd reinforced with a row of heavy rocks along the windowsill. The only open window was at the side of the room and gave onto a scrub-covered hillside.

There was another piece of plywood, which she used as a door when she slept, and when she was out for the day.

Her toiletries included a small tube of lotion, which she used only on her face. There was a new toothbrush. She used olive oil for the rest of her body and kept a tall bottle of it next to the toothpaste, separate from the one she used for work.

In another room, she'd made a larder along a cool wall—rock shelves of tomatoes, bread, and almonds in plastic bags, cheese, bottles of water. Peaches sometimes. Plums. Cucumbers.

For a while she'd marked days by leaving white pebbles on the windowsill when she returned home in the evenings, but soon she forgot, or lost interest in the measuring. They were still there, the first fourteen of them.

Each morning she walked along the dirt and up the asphalt, past the bus station, through the streets, along the marble walkway, past the church and its square to Anemomilos, where she entered through the arbor thick now with purple bougainvillea. And each morning she took her place at her same table, where, without being asked, the waitress brought a pot of coffee and touched Jacqueline's shoulder and said, "*Kalimera.*"

Sometimes, if she was in the mood, and if she'd done well on the beach the day before, she would order toast, or toast and eggs, but more often she'd have just the coffee. She'd take her time there in the mornings, watching other people eating their breakfasts, guests from the hotel taking their seats, families and couples and the occasional lone traveler like her.

Later she'd return through town and stop to sit on the square and watch the boys playing soccer, the whispering girls, the men spinning their beads, the gray women on their benches.

In the afternoons, she'd walk down to her beach and work. Sometimes she'd see the same people, but every few days there was a turnover and the faces would change. She made her money and swam and showered beneath the cold spray. Sometimes she'd buy a gyro in town and eat out on the wall of the fort. Other evenings she'd eat in her room.

And every morning, she went to see the waitress.

On one of those mornings the waitress said, "So what is her name? This woman I see every day. What is her name?" And she looked at Jacqueline with those narrow eyes. Those narrow eyes, which Jacqueline saw then were green, not brown. Eyes Jacqueline found lonely and familiar.

Jacqueline spoke her own name and before she could think, before she could stop herself, she asked, nearly laughing, "What is yours?"

"I am Katarina," the waitress said. Jacqueline fit the name to the woman and it was strange the way the name was applied to memory. It had been Katarina who served her breakfast that first morning in town, Katarina who brought the coffee, Katarina all along.

When she'd left that day, she felt joyous again. She walked through town and sat on the square and had to contain her grin so as not to appear a lunatic. She nodded and closed her eyes and replayed their exchange.

All that afternoon Jacqueline imagined the things she might ask Katarina, the ways she might begin a conversation of substance. A conversation, she thought at first, but what she wanted most of all was the two of them to sit somewhere and have a glass of wine and look out over some beautiful vista. How strange, she thought, that the only way into that kind of silence was through spoken language.

SO SHE'D RETURNED DAY AFTER DAY. *Kalimera*, Katarina. But for days and days, Jacqueline never had the courage, if that was what it was, to ask the simple questions she'd begun to collect in the night.

In the night when she'd whisper the questions aloud. The night when her mother whispered back. When she whispered, Maybe this is the reason, my heart. Maybe this is why you've come so far. To know this woman. Maybe this woman is the answer to all the questions. Perhaps what's happened to us is all for you to meet this woman. A long, difficult path here to this waitress.

When her mother whispered, Jacqueline couldn't sleep. The mattress screamed and screamed in her ears and she went and sat on the terrace, where she watched the shadow islands and listened to her heart thudding and the blood rushing through her head.

It was outrageous and insulting and it made her furious. Her mother's ideas. Her convenient thinking. Her foolish, childish notions. That those delirious boys were in her kitchen with their blades, all strung and strapped with their rifles, and that man in his beard and jackal eyes and all their biting hatred. That they had been there so that Jacqueline might come here to this girl, this waitress?

The idea was enraging. She couldn't sleep with it rattling in her head and yet her mother whispered it the way she'd once whispered, Good night, JaJa, my love, my heart, my little girl, and now in the dark when she was collecting questions, and trying to still herself for sleep, she couldn't ignore it and more infuriating was the possibility that her mother might be right.

Somehow and in spite of it all.

DAY AFTER DAY Jacqueline returned to the restaurant for her morning coffee and occasional breakfast and asked none of the questions she'd prepared.

Some days, she left Katarina and went down the steps, along the harbor, and out to the rocks. Sometimes one of the grill men would recognize her and wave. Sometimes some of the boys would smile at her on their way up to dive.

"Your father is impervious to beauty," her mother once said as if it were the greatest condemnation of all. She'd said it like it wasn't his fault. As if it were a condition he had no control over.

On good days, when she was free of the ferocious dark, of the weight and panic, she would try not to be impervious. On those days she swam with her eyes closed and lay on her warm rock and watched the sea as carefully as she could.

But those days were few and as the little village became more and more clogged with tourists, as the days grew longer and hotter, Jacqueline began to break her routine.

She woke later and later and even after she was awake, she lay in bed trying to ignore her mother's admonishing voice. Once, she woke so late that by the time she arrived at Anemomilos there were no open tables and she turned around and left. Other days she missed work and spent entire days in her sweltering room, where she watched the ceiling, dreaming of Bernard. Dreamed of making love, of him pressing down on her, and she dreamed of breaking his skull with a heavy rock.

And of the boys coming up the hill, coming up the hill, coming up the hill.

SHE FOUGHT AS BEST SHE COULD. She tried always to wake early, to always leave her room, to get to the restaurant, to sit in the square, to swim, to work, to bathe, to brush her teeth, to keep things tidy, to follow her routine, to keep her life. But sometimes she could not.

Sometimes she betrayed herself. Or her mind betrayed her. Or her body.

Sometimes her mind was brutal, was vicious, was unrelenting.

Sometimes the flashing behind her closed eyes was dizzying.

Sometimes she wanted to drive a knife into her brain.

Sometimes the sound of it all, the flashing images, her mother's voice, the voice of her father, the sight of Saifa's feet, the feeling of them in her hands, the conflation of present life and memory, of what existed and did not, sometimes the pressure of it, the noise, the volume and weight, was too much to sleep, to eat, to breathe and, she began to wonder, if it wasn't too much to live.

But she fought.

Even if she felt she was losing, she fought.

And then after days of not leaving her room, of not eating, of surviving on sips of water from a tall plastic bottle, of sweating in her bed, of pissing in another room, of defecating in yet another, two days of horrific dreams she could never remember, days of crushing weight, of her mother's eyes, her father's weeping, her sister's silent bleeding, days of madness and muttering to herself and scratching at her wrists, and incessant noise, there was a crash of silence and Jacqueline fell finally to sleep.

WHEN SHE WOKE very early the next morning, she was alert and she was still and the only noise she heard was the soft sound of wind rushing off the water and up the valley. She dressed and walked the road into town and arrived at the restaurant weak and dizzy.

The terrace was empty when Jacqueline found her table.

"*Kalimera,* Jacqueline."

"*Kalimera,* Katarina."

She was holding a tray of silverware sets rolled in white napkins.

"Early today."

She nodded and looked away. Katarina put her tray on the table and sat down and covered Jacqueline's hand with hers.

"You are well?"

"A little tired," she said, the admission feeling like some tremendous revelation.

"Yes, I can see."

There was a moment of quiet, Katarina's hand on Jacqueline's.

"Well, I'll bring you your coffee, yes?"

Jacqueline nodded. She was afraid to speak, afraid her voice would betray her.

Katarina returned with the coffee and a plate of scrambled eggs and a basket of toast and a glass of orange juice. She put the food in front of Jacqueline and then sat down. There were two cups and Katarina poured coffee for them both.

"Eat," Katarina said. "Please."

Jacqueline smiled. She shook her head. She'd begun to cry and could not look up.

"Please," Katarina said, returning her soft hand to Jacqueline's, covering the dry scab.

"Please," Katarina said.

Jacqueline unrolled the silverware and unfolded the napkin and spread it across her lap.

"Please."

She could not look up, but she began to eat the eggs.

Katarina spread butter across a piece of toast and laid it gently on the edge of the plate. She added cream and sugar to Jacqueline's coffee.

"Enough?" she asked, and Jacqueline nodded.

She fought them as hard as she could, but tears were running down her cheeks and dripping into her eggs and soon she gave up. She put her fork down, and raised the sheer paper napkin from her lap, and pressed it to her face. All of her control was gone. She cried with a violence that made it difficult for her to breathe or swallow. She could feel Katarina's hand tighten around her own.

"Breathe, please," she said. "Breathe."

And slowly she was able to get a breath. Slowly she stopped crying.

"Here," Katarina said. "Here," and Jacqueline opened her eyes.

Katarina was holding a fresh napkin out to her. She took it.

"I'm sorry."

"No. Please," Katarina said, pushing Jacqueline's hand toward the plate. "Please. Please, you must eat. It is getting cold."

Jacqueline nodded and raised her fork and ate some of the eggs. She could feel the hunger returning and would have eaten faster had it not been for Katarina, whose eyes she was still ashamed to meet.

"Some toast, please," Katarina said.

Jacqueline laughed then and nearly spit her eggs out of her mouth. She shook her head and finally, finally, she looked up.

Katarina nodded and pushed the coffee toward her and said, "Now, please."

Jacqueline drank some of the coffee.

Katarina drank some of hers.

"What is it?" Katarina asked.

Jacqueline wanted to answer. She wanted to say what it was. She wanted to tell her everything that it was. Instead she shook her head and took a bite of toast. Her hunger came and went, came and went.

"You are American?"

"No." Jacqueline shook her head.

"No? I thought you were American."

"No. Liberian."

Katarina nodded. "I don't know this country."

"In Africa."

"And your name? It is like Mrs. Kennedy."

Jacqueline smiled. "Yes. My namesake."

"Yes. I think you are elegant like her."

Jacqueline smiled and shook her head. "My father's idea. He was a great admirer of America, and of the Kennedys."

Katarina nodded. "My mother was the same. She loved her very much."

Jacqueline could feel her heart slowing. She took a first full breath.

"I was born at JFK Hospital," Jacqueline said.

"In Liberia?"

"Yes."

Katarina nodded. "And your friends call you Jackie?"

Jacqueline looked away. "No."

"Nobody calls you Jackie?"

"Nobody," Jacqueline said.

Katarina nodded.

"I will leave you to finish."

"I'm sorry. I didn't mean to be short."

"Short?"

"Rude."

"No. I ask many questions. You should eat. You should finish everything." She stood up from the table. "And I should work. Please, you should finish everything."

Jacqueline smiled. "Yes, I will."

Katarina tapped the table once with the four fingers of her left hand, crossed the terrace, and disappeared into the building.

Everything had cooled—the eggs, the coffee, the toast—but she finished it all. And then she drank the orange juice and afterward sat slumped in her chair, exhausted and embarrassed and disappointed.

She watched Katarina finish laying the tables. She watched the terrace become crowded with people and still she didn't move, didn't signal for the bill, nothing. Eventually Katarina came over and sat down again, this time sideways, half at the table and half gone. Just like the tall man in his restaurant all that time ago.

"Jacqueline," she said softly, as if she were coaxing a stubborn child. "Jacqueline, is there anything more you need?"

She sat up and came back to herself then, and smiled and said, "No. No. Nothing. I'm fine. Just the check. I'm sorry. I'm sorry." She wanted to go on, and explain one thing and make another clear, but nothing more came to her, so she finished by shaking her head and reaching for her pack, which lay beneath the table at her feet.

"There's no charge today. Today there's no charge."

"No, no," Jacqueline said, bringing the pack up to her lap and unzipping the top pocket.

"Please," Katarina said, reaching out and squeezing Jacqueline's wrist, stilling her.

"No," Jacqueline said again, this time more sharply. And pulled her wrist away. She felt a sense of panic then, the very panic she'd felt as a girl after slapping Saifa harder than she'd meant to. Again she said, "I'm sorry."

Katarina leaned forward and said very quietly, but with force, "Today there is no charge, but you will make it up tonight. This evening you can buy me a glass of something. This evening, okay. Okay?"

Jacqueline looked up and said yes, she would do that. "Yes, okay."

"Good. Now I am going to work."

"What time?" Jacqueline said.

"Six. Here at six."

She nodded and collected her things, and when Katarina had gone to serve another table, she left the restaurant and walked out onto the street, feeling bewildered and dazed and distant from herself, from the world around her.

She came to the square and found her place and sat watching the same two teenage girls. They were smoking cigarettes with exaggerated, theatrical gestures, like cartoons, like little cartoon women, Jacqueline thought, waving their hands around and throwing their heads back to exhale smoke into the air.

She watched and felt such a strong affection for them, she worried she would cry again.

She looked out over the caldera.

Jacqueline and Helen walked together through Hampstead Heath, the two of them smoking cigarettes, drunk, days before they'd have to return to school.

Helen ran ahead of her. She was turning now, her arms extended. Jacqueline could see her face. Cheeks red from the gin and the cold, Helen lowered her head and pawed the grass with her foot. She made horns with her fingers and squinted her blue eyes. Jacqueline pulled the white scarf from her neck and shook it. Toro. Toro.

Her mother raised her eyes, but said nothing.

She'd made a fool of herself. Weeping like that in front of a stranger, accepting free food again like a beggar. And with plenty of money to pay for it. She shook her head. She looked at herself at that table, crying, holding the napkin to her face. Idiot, she thought. Pathetic. She stood and crossed the walkway and leaned on the wall and looked down at a cruise ship moving across the water.

Bernard had called her Jackie. She heard him whispering it, the French inflected emphasis on the second syllable. Ja. *Key.* He was the only one. "Jackie," he said. "One day, you'll come and live with me in Nice." They were sitting together. She couldn't remember where exactly, but she remembered a plastic table, plastic chairs. Some little restaurant on a beach. Somewhere out of town. She could see his slender fingers, could see his clean fingernails. He had a slim stack of Polaroids bound with a rubber band, which he'd removed and was now dealing onto the table. "Jackie, look," he said. They were pictures of the beach in Nice, of cafés, of his ugly sister, of his happy friends. And then a series of photos of his apartment, which faced the sea and had a balcony with a metal table and chairs where he said they would eat breakfast together every morning, where they'd drink pastis in the evening before going out to dinner.

He was trying to convince her then, to come and live with him. In those early days, before everything turned, including Bernard himself, and the country went even madder, and he'd become disgusted with it, and then with her because he was incapable of separating her from it, or her from them. He was trying to convince her to leave, to come live in his airy apartment on the sea, with its blue shutters and balcony, and the beautiful promenade below. "There you can go to university," he said. "There you can do what you like."

Now she could hear his voice, but it was the voice of some other man.

"I'll be done here soon. They'll bring me home. You'll come with me. Our beaches are easier to sell." He laughed. "Much easier to sell."

But this was early on, before he'd understood. This was when Ghankay's crimes were abstractions to him, to them both. It was before he'd begun to leave the city, before he'd begun to travel, before he'd seen those boys training in the jungle. Before he'd seen them do the things they'd trained to do. Before he'd seen them tear the intestines out of living men and drag them through the dirt, before he saw them cut the hearts out of living men, before he saw them eat their hearts, their testicles. Before he saw them laugh, and paint themselves with blood, and pound their own intact chests and dance with the power, and fire their rifles in the air.

Before that, he showed her photographs of his apartment in Nice with its great white bed and the sheer curtains billowing in the wind and he said, "Come live with me, Jackie," and he put his charming emphasis on the last syllable of her name.

And after, though he never said it, she was certain. She knew he could no longer separate her from them. It was all the same thing. Jacqueline, and her father, and Ghankay, and her mother, and the boys in the jungle coming closer, day after day. Coming for blood, coming for the city. She'd been a fool for returning home, a fool for staying.

And there were times she thought he might be right, that there was no difference.

He never said it, but she saw him look at her, and she knew. She knew, and she let him save her life anyway. In Sierra Leone, she let him guide her through the airport by her elbow, let him put her on that plane, let him clear his precious, fickle, and liquid conscience, let him wash his hands of her.

Now, as she stood at the wall watching the great ship inch across the water toward the harbor at Fira, she could hear him thinking.

I have done my duty. I have saved her life. I am free of her, of them, of that miserable, wasted place. I am free and I have done more than most men.

She could see him standing on his precious balcony.

She stood with him. She touched his hand and together they looked down on the promenade and across the sand and out to the bay and through the sea, past Cagliari and Bizerte, between Ragusa and Malta, past Crete to this cliff. To this wall, this worn marble path where she stood alone.

To this island where she lived.

———————

SHE WAS RESTLESS and began to walk farther into town. She asked a man standing in front of a jewelry shop, spinning his worry beads, for the time. She asked without hesitation, without thinking, and he responded easily and without suspicion.

It was a few minutes after noon. The time seemed to have been sucked away. It felt as if she'd been at the restaurant so long ago. She continued out to the fort, where she climbed over the ramparts and sat with her back to the wall. She watched the islands change color as they passed in and out of cloud shade.

This is what you wanted, her mother said. Someone to see in the evenings. Someone to sit with.

Yes, Jacqueline said.

Remember the handsome men on the square? Remember the women, the children admiring your footwork? Your cup of coffee on its saucer?

Jacqueline nodded.

You remember all of that?

Yes.

Well, then. Why do you hesitate?

Jacqueline didn't know.

You're just like him, her mother said. She'd torn a hangnail and was now leaning against the kitchen counter, sucking the blood from her little finger.

Jacqueline could see her so clearly. Head to the side, squinting in some combination of pain and concentration, her cheeks drawn up. No, not pain, that kind of sting didn't even register as pain to her mother. It was irritation. A combination of irritation and concentration.

You're just like him, she repeated. He preferred the fantasy. Always. Both of you. You'd rather sit in the dark and wish. Stubborn, stupid, and blind.

Jacqueline nodded.

Do you know what I think, JaJa? I think he was surprised. I think he was surprised up until the very moment those boys arrived. Maybe beyond that. Maybe he was surprised until the very moment he died. Maybe he's *still* surprised. That's how stupid he was. Do you know what he said to me once? *Him?* Do you know what *he* told *me?* Fantasy is a kind of stupidity, he said. Fantasy is a kind of stupidity.

"Fantasy is a kind of stupidity," Jacqueline repeated. They were talking on the telephone. Jacqueline was in her room, looking out across the playing fields covered in snow.

"Your father so loyal to that man. What greater fantasy in the world than the fantasy of Ghankay's goodness."

"Yes," Jacqueline had said. "Yes."

She could hear the ice in the glass.

If you go and hide in your room, her mother said now, if you lock yourself away, or go on to one of those islands there, you'll never forgive yourself. You'll never forgive yourself and you'll never recover, do you understand me? Never.

Jacqueline nodded.

Do you trust her?

She did.

Then you will go at six. You will go at six and meet her. You are not a child. You are not a little girl. You may not hide in your room. You may not.

Jacqueline could see her mother furious, drunk, standing at the front of the house, her feet bare, dressed in her nightgown, panting, having just flung a glass at the back of her husband's car, having missed entirely, the gate whirring closed.

You may not, her mother said again.

Some other night, a night that rose out of her memory, some night when Jacqueline had been crying, and her gentle mother sat beside her on the bed, holding her warm palm firm and sure against Jacqueline's chest, firm just below her throat, pressing away the pain.

Someone had been cruel to her.

"Shhh," her mother had whispered. "You're better than that, my heart. You're in another world, my love. Another stratosphere. Those people"—whoever they were—"they do not exist for you. Not for you. Not for us."

Jacqueline left the fort and wandered the village, browsing through postcards and magazines. She went into a shop that sold expensive strands of worry beads and held them in her hand. The saleswoman glanced up and then returned to her book.

Jacqueline went into an art gallery that smelled of incense and looked at dramatic black-and-white photographs that did no justice to the island.

She held cheap worry beads in her hand at a tourist shop and for a moment thought she might buy herself some. She loved so much the way they sounded in the evenings spinning over the shopkeepers' knuckles.

JaJa, her mother said sharply.

Jacqueline sighed and returned them to the rack.

She spent the day like that, like a tourist, a proper tourist on holiday, taking time from another life.

Eventually she returned to the square, where she sat and watched people passing and the kids playing soccer and the two girls on their bench. She eavesdropped when the conversations were in English, and as the light changed, she returned to herself sitting at the table that morning with the napkin covering her face, making a fool of herself. She imagined packing her things, leaving her room, returning to Fira, or to some other town, or to a ferry for some other island, but by then it was too late and she knew she wouldn't leave, that her mother was right, that the only thing to do now was to return to Anemomilos.

And this was a kind of deciding.

The afternoon drifted away from her. She moved in and out of reverie. She listened to her mother and watched Saifa on the sand. She looked across the table at her father and felt the pleasure of his attention, and she felt the pressure of Bernard's thigh against hers, and as it grew later, she listened to the muted otherworldly acoustics of the caldera shell. She saw the shopkeepers standing stoic in their doorways spinning their beads over and over and over their open hands, the round old women minding their fierce children who chased the village dogs, and played soccer in front of the church.

She watched a priest in a long gray beard and black robes, and a heavy cross around his neck traverse the square like a spirit and unlock the church doors and draw them open and disappear inside. For a moment she wasn't certain if her eyes were open or closed, if the man existed in her present life or if he was of memory, or hallucination. But he was there gliding across the tiles, feet hidden by his robes.

She closed her eyes and saw the restaurants and their tea lights sparkling, the handsome waiters pouring cold wine into delicate glasses, using round, water-smoothed stones to keep napkins from blowing out to the sea in which the moon cast its copper light. She saw all the perfect paths leading to all the white hotels spreading down the cliff, all the way down to the edge where it fell away too steep to build, and all their modest swimming pools incandescent, lit from within, kidneys and rectangles, glass beads of washed-out blue and green, and the old fort at the very end of the village and its low walls and barely a light there so that two people warm from the sun, hair still damp, might stand above it all in the dark and feel the wind cooling their skin.

JACQUELINE STOOD UP and approached the two girls. They were turned inward on the bench, facing each other, sharing a cigarette, laughing, lost in their stories, and when they were aware of Jacqueline standing above them, they changed into adults and turned their eyes upward, adopting a collective expression of cool maturity.

Jacqueline asked if they spoke English and when they said they did, she asked the time, and when they gave it to her—twenty minutes to six—she smiled.

"Thank you," she said. "*Kalimera.*"

The girls laughed and said in unison, "*Kalispera.*"

"Oh," Jacqueline said. "I'm sorry. *Kalispera* is good evening?"

"Yes," they said again in unison, like a little choir, and smiled at her as if she were a child.

She raised her hand and waved. "*Kalispera,*" she said and walked away to Anemomilos, where she paused a moment beneath the arbor before stepping onto the terrace, her vision sharp, her heart beating hard.

Jacqueline had never been to the restaurant in the evening. The soft yellow light laid long shadows across the tables and cut through the shuddering trellis flowers. There were two women, both with loose gray hair falling around their shoulders, at one of the tables still in the sun. Otherwise, the place was empty. She thought of walking into the restaurant, but the prospect of entering that building to find Katarina was daunting, so she sat at her table and waited and watched the women with their eyes closed and the light cutting through their glasses of beer. There were identical red packs slung over the backs of their chairs.

She glanced over at the building.

Saifa moved across the lawn, feet hidden by her dress.

The cat was gone.

The cat had known better.

And before any of them.

Katarina moved across the terrace. She wore a light blue dress cut at the knee and brown leather sandals, and her hair down. She looked showered and bright and strode toward the table with an unfamiliar energy. In her right hand she carried a wide white scarf.

Jacqueline felt humiliated again, and wished that she'd gone down to the beach and showered, put some lotion on her face, and rubbed her legs with olive oil.

She could feel her muscles contract as if she were about to get up, turn, and leave.

Stay where you are, her mother said. Smile. Breathe. This is what people do. They meet. They talk. They drink, they share food. They look at each other.

Jacqueline nodded.

Katarina stopped and leaned over to talk to the women. She touched one of them on the arm. The three of them laughed.

God's will, her mother said. This long path. This woman. All we've given up to be here. All the faith. In spite of yourself. In spite of me. Like it or not. You are what's left of us.

Katarina stood up straight. Her mouth was moving, but wind was taking all the sound away.

You smile. You breathe. You speak. It is what people do, JaJa. Even if you can't remember, it is what they do. It'll come back, my heart. Trust me, my love. Trust me. Trust God.

She nodded.

Katarina turned.

Jacqueline raised her chin. She drew in a deep breath. She smiled.

"Jacqueline," Katarina said when she was close enough. "Jacqueline," she said again, fighting the wind, pushing her hair away from her eyes, tucking a strand behind her left ear.

And Jacqueline rose up, straightened her back, and said, "*Kali*spera, Katarina. *Kalispera*."

She felt Katarina's hand on her shoulder and then her cheek against hers.

"*Kali*spera, to you. I'm impressed. Come on. We're going now," and Katarina pulled gently on Jacqueline's arm.

Then they were walking together across the terrace and across the street, and instead of turning toward town as Jacqueline had expected they would, they turned up the lava rock path, with its low, steadily rising steps and began to walk in the direction of the rose church. Katarina had hooked Jacqueline's arm with hers and they moved together now. She knew that this too might be a kind of charity, the relentless enthusiasm of the philanthropist, but whatever it was she'd already begun to give in and there was unmistakable joy in this physical closeness, in abandoning herself to someone else's control.

Again she was being led.

"So, you have learned Greek since this morning?"

"Some girls taught me. Teenagers on the square today. So now I have two words."

"I will teach you the other two tonight."

Jacqueline laughed.

To their right, all the houses and hotels lay below the steepening path on the cliff side, so that the view to the water from where they walked was unobscured and they could look down past the roofs and terraces and swimming pools and out to the still sea. The sky was turning pink and for a moment Jacqueline imagined all the tourists collected at the end of the village to watch the earth turn away from the sun.

"Here," Katarina said and brought them to a stop in front of a wooden gate painted white, each picket tipped with gray. A low orange light hooded in metal illuminated a vertical porcelain plaque fixed to the white concrete wall.

"Look." Katarina pointed to the smooth rooftop below.

There were four dogs curled up together asleep.

"In the evening they take the heat that's left from the day."

The two women watched the dogs for a moment.

"I met a dog here," Jacqueline said. "But he disappeared."

Katarina opened the gate and they walked down a flight of wide steps, each of which was painted gray and edged in white.

They came around a turn, and now Jacqueline saw a rectangular swimming pool lit green and sunk in the heart of a concrete terrace painted the same storm gray. There were five small empty tables around the pool, each with a lit candle in a hurricane lantern.

Jacqueline exhaled in surprise.

"Pretty, no?"

"Beautiful," Jacqueline said. "It's a restaurant?"

"A hotel."

She followed Katarina down.

"Sit, please."

Jacqueline did.

"I'm right back. I will go for our drinks."

Jacqueline, hypnotized by the place, nodded, and when Katarina had gone, she looked at the white candle guttering behind the glass, and then at the green pool, and out at the fading pink sky and at the water beneath it, a vast sheet of steel.

She sat back in her chair and took a first full breath.

You see? her mother said. God.

"Shhh," Jacqueline said aloud. "Shhh."

IV

WHEN KATARINA RETURNS she takes the chair next to Jacqueline so that they both have the same view.

"He is coming," she says, and Jacqueline doesn't ask who. They're both quiet as the sky turns purple.

A small brown dog trots down the steps and around the edge of the pool. It sniffs at Jacqueline's knees. She leans forward and takes its head between her hands and scratches its ears.

"I love them," Katarina says. "I would like to keep them all."

"Me too," Jacqueline says.

"Yes? That's good. There are many people who don't feel the same as us. Many of the people hate them."

"My sister," Jacqueline says, "always preferred cats."

Katarina glances at her and nods.

"But I have always loved dogs."

I should shut my mouth, Jacqueline thinks.

Relax, her mother says. Be easy, my heart. Be easy.

The dog swings its head over to Katarina, nuzzles her hand, and then heads toward the entrance of the hotel.

"These people think that dogs are dangerous for the tourists."

Jacqueline nods.

"They feed them glass," Katarina says and tightens her mouth.

"They what?"

"Yes. They put little pieces in the food and feed it to the dogs so they go to die very, very slow. Yes. They do that, these people."

Jacqueline turns away and looks back at the sky, which has become nearly all its night-blue.

A man comes out of the building carrying a tray. He's barefoot, dressed in white pants and a black T-shirt.

"*Kalispera*," he says to Jacqueline. He has short-cropped gray hair and tired blue eyes.

Jacqueline nods. "*Kalispera*," she says.

He begins to unload the contents of the tray and says something to Katarina in Greek.

"This is Petros. My father's friend. He is the owner here."

"*Kalispera*," Jacqueline says again.

The man smiles, bows his head, and leaves them.

"You should learn the other two words," Katarina says.

"*Kalispera*," Jacqueline says and Katarina laughs.

On the table there is a white bowl piled with ice cubes. There are two small white plates. One full of almonds, the other full of fat green olives. There is a bottle of water and two empty glasses, and a bottle of clear alcohol.

"Like this," Katarina says. She uncorks the alcohol and pours them each two fingers. She spoons ice cubes into each of their glasses. Then she adds water, which turns the mixture from clear to clouded yellow.

"Ouzo," she says.

"Ouzo," Jacqueline says and raises her glass.

Katarina laughs. "No, it *is* ouzo."

"Ah," Jacqueline says.

"*Yiamas*," Katarina says.

"*Yiamas*," Jacqueline repeats.

They touch glasses and drink.

She loves the cool sweetness, the licorice on her tongue, the burn of the alcohol in her throat, the ice against her lips. She swallows and returns her glass to the table.

"Delicious," she says. "Ouzo."

"Ouzo," Katarina repeats, picks up the bowl of olives, and offers Jacqueline one. "Be careful," she says. "They have rocks."

"Stones," Jacqueline says.

"Stones," Katarina repeats.

Thank you for bringing me here, Jacqueline wants to say. Thank you for taking care of me, but while she feels the words on her tongue, she can't push them out.

Instead she says, "Or pits."

The wind has come up again and snaps at the white tablecloths. Katarina unfolds her scarf and wraps it around her shoulders.

"Often cold nights here. You have nothing?"

Jacqueline shrugs. "I'm fine."

Katarina nods, but when she sees Petros cross the terrace she calls something to him and a minute later he is striding toward them, unfolding a thin gray blanket, which he silently wraps around Jacqueline's shoulders.

"*Efkharistó*, Petros," Katarina says.

And Jacqueline repeats the sentence. "*Efkharistó*, Petros," she calls after him as he walks away.

Katarina smiles. "Now you have all four words."

Jacqueline laughs. "It means thank you?"

"Thank you."

"*Efkharistó*, Katarina," Jacqueline says and meets her eyes.

"It is you who is buying me the drink tonight."

Jacqueline laughs. "Yes. True."

"So. You are better now?"

Jacqueline pulls the soft blanket around her shoulders. "Yes," she says. "Much better."

"No, I mean better than this morning. You are better than this morning."

"Oh. Yes. Yes," Jacqueline says. "Yes."

"It was your sister?"

Jacqueline glances at Katarina and then out at the water. This is not what she wants, this conversation. What she wants is to drink and be still and watch the sky change and the boats come and go.

Go on, her mother says. Go on, my heart.

"Yes," she says.

"And she is gone?"

Jacqueline gives her a quick slashing look.

Katarina opens her mouth. She looks as if she's been slapped. "I'm sorry," she says.

Easy, my heart.

"No," Jacqueline says to the moon, which is just drawing up over the far cliffs of Imerovigli. "Don't be sorry."

She glances back at Katarina and then at once sees how young she is, how easy she would be to damage.

"Don't be sorry," Jacqueline says again. "It's just. I am," she begins, but doesn't finish the sentence. Instead, although they both have plenty, she pours more of the ouzo, adds ice, adds water. She raises her glass and by way of apology says, "Ouzo."

Katarina looks over and opens her mouth to correct Jacqueline, but when she sees Jacqueline smiling, Katarina laughs and they clink glasses. "Ouzo," she repeats and they both drink.

"My sister is dead," Jacqueline says after she returns her glass to the white cloth.

She feels the violence of that statement. It is a weapon. She's struck the girl with it. That's not what she meant, she thinks. But it *is* what she meant. She wanted to crush this pretty idiot girl with it. My sister is dead and that's not all. That's just the start, so shut your mouth. But she can hear her mother clicking her tongue in disapproval and Jacqueline knows she's right so she says it again, this time without malice.

"My sister is dead," she says gently. And now she has said it twice. Twice in her life. She feels light-headed for a moment. She takes some almonds from the bowl and chews them. They are tasteless in her mouth.

Katarina nods and, thank God, doesn't say she's sorry, doesn't touch Jacqueline, doesn't give her a look of contrived sympathy. Katarina only nods, and raises her glass to her lips and the two women sit together watching the moon, which has lost its color as it's risen, fading from orange, to yellow, to this iridescent white tinged with blue.

Jacqueline lowers her eyes and watches the terrace wall's sharp-edged shadow.

She watches Saifa turn and face the house, Saifa walk across the lawn, her hands on her belly, long fingers inter-laced. She tries to walk with confidence, but it's no good, and from where Jacqueline sits in the living room, she can see her sister's posture weakening. She's folding forward, inch by inch, over her own belly. Like a set of jaws closing down on a fat plum. For a moment, Jacqueline thinks it's to do with the baby. Maybe it's now, she thinks and stands up quickly from the couch, upsetting the stack of magazines on her lap and dropping them to the floor. But then she stops herself. She can hear voices coming up the hill. She can hear a metal sound. Someone's shaking the fence, rattling the chain link against its posts.

Saifa turns her head and looks in the direction of the noise.

Jacqueline watches her sister's face.

The laughter is louder and louder.

Jacqueline watches Saifa faint and fall to the grass, her head bouncing off the soft ground and still Jacqueline doesn't move. She stands in the living room gaping through the open doors, glossy magazines at her feet, throat dry. She sees them there on the floor. Those vacant glittering eyes. *Vogue. Elle.* Then she recovers and begins to move. She crosses the living room, goes through the sliding doors, and steps out onto the concrete deck. From here she can see across the yard to her left, to the fence, where there is now a mass of soldiers. They are boys and they are grinning and when Jacqueline steps into their line of view, their faces light up, and then they brighten again. Like one of those three-step bulbs. Bright, brighter, brightest.

Jacqueline looks back. She turns her body in their direction, as if she alone might ward them off. And meanwhile her sister, a few steps away, is coming to, is sitting up.

"Go inside, Saifa," Jacqueline says, watching the grinning boys, who've become still and quiet at the fence. She knows it won't be long. Despite the razor wire. The guards are gone.

They're all that's left now. The four of them.

And then the man with the beard rises.

He comes up the hill.

Now she can only see him. He's looking at her, his lips slightly parted. She can only see him. His straight white teeth. He raises a pistol and levels it.

"Inside," he says. "Back inside." He flicks the pistol to his right.

And Jacqueline obeys him. She obeys him immediately. She walks backward into the house until he vanishes.

———

KATARINA SAYS, "I'm sorry for your sister."

Jacqueline nods. "Thank you."

"Was she older?"

"Older?"

"More than you," Katarina says, gently rattling the ice in her glass.

"No," Jacqueline says.

"Younger?"

"Younger."

Katarina nods.

Jacqueline swallows and feels the light burn of the alcohol in her throat.

"She was sick? My mother was sick."

Jacqueline looks over at the girl. She looks back. She seems so young, so frightened. Jacqueline is drunk. She could crush Katarina. And she wants to. She wants to beat her with what she knows. She wants to scream at her. What I have to say, little girl. The things I have to say. She wants to deliver them with violence. But she waits for it to pass. She waits because she does not want to hurt this girl, her waitress, her nurse.

"No," Jacqueline says. "She wasn't sick."

"Wasn't sick," Katarina repeats quietly.

Jacqueline laughs and Katarina looks at her, incredulous. "You laugh? Why?"

Jacqueline shakes her head. "I don't know."

"You don't?"

"The ouzo," Jacqueline says. "Maybe it's the ouzo."

She'll think you're crazy, her mother says.

She'll be right, Jacqueline says, spooning more ice into her glass and stirring it.

"Yes, I feel it also," Katarina says and forces a weak smile.

"Ouzo," Jacqueline says, raising her glass.

"Ouzo," Katarina repeats.

They touch glasses, but the joke is worn.

Jacqueline has disappointed the girl. Katarina too must have had expectations, must have imagined their evening together, their friendship even. Perhaps.

She has rendered her caretaker impotent.

"Do you want to know?" Jacqueline asks, without thinking first.

She asks to fill the silence.

The girl looks over at Jacqueline. "If you will tell me. If you want only," she says, brightening.

"What happened to your mother?" Jacqueline asks.

"Cancer," the girl says without hesitation, as if she's eager to say it, as if she's been waiting for the question, impatient.

Jacqueline nods and sees Katarina at her mother's bedside, pressing a cool washcloth to the woman's forehead. Day after day she's there. Loyal, loving daughter.

The image makes Jacqueline angry. She feels no sympathy and looks away from the girl and out to the water.

Why, my heart? her mother asks. Why would you be angry?

She says nothing and waits for it to pass.

And when it does, she says, "I'm sorry, Katarina," although she is not.

Now they are both quiet.

Then Jacqueline can feel Katarina looking at her and reluctantly she meets the girl's eyes. She's surprised to find them angry.

The girl expected more, of course. More information. More intimacy. More compassion.

"How old are you, Katarina?" She's careful not to be condescending, careful to avoid a tone of superiority, but she's not sure if she succeeds.

"I am twenty-one," she says and raises her chin, looking at Jacqueline as if to say, So what? So what?

"And *you*?" the girl asks in return. Insolent.

Jacqueline laughs and looks away. She feels as if they're becoming children. If we go on like this we'll be teenagers before too long. Then our feet won't reach the floor. She smiles at the idea. The two of them, little girls dressed up like women, getting drunk on ouzo.

A tea party with white candles.

"Why do you laugh?" Katarina asks, scratching at her cheek.

"Oh," Jacqueline says, "I just imagined us as little girls." She tells the truth. Just speaks.

"Little girls?" Katarina raises her eyes.

She shakes her head. "It was just a flash. Just. I should probably stop the ouzo."

"Why little girls?"

She shakes her head. "I don't know."

Katarina raises her eyebrows.

"I don't know. I just imagined it. Our legs sticking out. Little girls dressed up like women."

Katarina looks away. "You are strange," she says.

Jacqueline nods.

"You are strange and you are sad."

After a moment Jacqueline says, "Perhaps. Perhaps those things are both true."

Perhaps, her father says.

"And you? You are how old?"

"Twenty-four."

"*So.* Not so much older than me."

"No."

"Are you married?" Katarina asks.

"No."

"No, neither am I."

Petros crosses the terrace. He addresses them both in Greek.

Katarina turns to Jacqueline. "Would you like to eat something?"

Jacqueline nods. "Yes," she says. Again not thinking.

Katarina and Petros talk and then he's gone.

Jacqueline has forgotten herself. Forgotten about money. Then for a long moment she cannot recall where she sleeps at night, where she leaves her things. She closes her eyes and does her best not to summon that memory, but in spite of the ouzo it comes.

There's the shell of a hotel.

There are her rocks for shelves.

There are her peaches lined up in the larder.

"How did your mother die?" Jacqueline asks.

"I have told you," Katarina says, exasperated.

"I mean," Jacqueline says. "I mean what was the kind of cancer?" She sounds like Katarina now, shuffling words, replacing adjectives with verbs, nouns with adjectives.

"Breast."

"I'm sorry."

The girl looks at Jacqueline, gauges her eyes, and then looks away.

"When did she die?"

"*Fevrouários.*"

Somewhere music begins to play. Distorted and thin in the wind. Strings. Something with strings, Jacqueline thinks. The sound rises and fades and rises again.

"What was she like?"

The girl shakes her head. "It is strange," she says. "I don't know. I don't know what was she like."

Jacqueline looks over at her.

"I have been thinking that all the time since she died. I don't know what was she like." She shakes her head again and says nothing more.

The wind dies down and the rushing is replaced by the strings.

"Music," Jacqueline says.

They're both still. Listening.

"A bouzouki," Katarina says.

"Pretty."

"My father plays. He is very good."

Jacqueline glances over at the girl and wants to hold her. She looks so proud. Jacqueline wants to take her in her arms. You'll be fine, she wants to say. You're safe now. You're safe.

"*Mana mou,*" Jacqueline says.

Katarina looks at her and smiles. "You know this?"

"Yes."

"How?"

"I can't remember." Jacqueline shakes her head. She can't remember where the phrase comes from. How has it come to be in her memory? Where did she learn it? Still, she wants to comfort the girl.

"My mother too, Katarina. My mother too is dead."

Katarina turns in her chair. "Your mother?"

Jacqueline nods.

"Your mother and your sister. Both."

"Yes."

"And both were not sick."

"No."

Jacqueline turns away from the moon and meets Katarina's eyes. "They were not sick."

You have said it, her mother whispers. Tender. You have said it, her mother says, this time louder.

You have killed me.

Katarina moves and Jacqueline is afraid that she'll touch her, but she only uncrosses and crosses her legs so that she has shifted her body entirely in Jacqueline's direction.

"They were together?"

Jacqueline nods. She wishes the food would come. She's too drunk. She's ravenous. She wonders what Petros will bring on his tray. She hopes it is meat. Suddenly she wants meat more than anything.

"Jacqueline," Katarina says.

"What?" She has faded from the table, but here is this girl jerking her back.

"They were together?" Katarina asks again.

Jacqueline is irritated. She's hot. She can't stand the table or its flickering candle, or the olives. She wants a plate of meat. She wants to throw her chair over the cliff edge. She can feel it in her hands. She can see it spinning in the dark. She'd like to throw all the tables into the pool. Smash all the delicate glass lanterns against the concrete deck.

She gets out of her chair and walks to the edge and looks down to the rocks and water far below.

Jacqueline braces for Katarina's hand on her shoulder, but it doesn't come, and when she turns around to face the girl, she finds her still in her chair with her elbows on the table, cheek in one hand, glass in the other, watching Jacqueline.

"Yes," Jacqueline says. "They were together. We were all together."

She can feel the vast dark space at her back.

"All?"

She nods and returns to her chair and slumps down. She is so hungry. She shouldn't have drunk so much so quickly. She's never had her mother's tolerance, and now on an empty stomach, now after not drinking for so long. She tries to remember the last time she drank alcohol.

"Once," Jacqueline says, "a long time ago. I was a girl. Very young. Ten years old, maybe. We were on vacation. The Canary Islands. Not so far away from here. We were sitting by the pool and I ordered a Coke from the waiter. When it came, it tasted strange, but I thought it was just the way Coke tasted there and so I didn't mention it to my mom until I'd finished most of it. They'd brought me a rum and Coke."

Katarina smiles. "You were sick?"

Jacqueline shakes her head. "I don't remember. I just thought of that story."

The ice in the bowl has turned to water.

Jacqueline knows that she has not answered Katarina's question. She can hear it hanging in the air. The wind blows the bouzouki music away. And then there is Petros striding toward them, carrying a tray. He lays all the food out on the table. He names each dish as he puts it down.

The plates surround the hurricane lantern. Most of it she doesn't recognize, but the stuffed peppers she does. She thinks of that meal.

Of that table.

Its shade.

Of that man so long ago.

She recognizes the peppers and the skewers of meat. She looks at it all and then up at Katarina, who is smiling at her.

"Eat," she says. "Please."

Be polite, her mother says.

Petros returns with a bottle of wine and two glasses in one hand, a bucket of ice in the other. "Askyrtiko," he says, pours them each a glass, twists the bottle into the ice, and leaves them.

"Askyrtiko. A local wine," Katarina says. "Very good." She raises her glass. "Ouzo," she says and smiles.

"Ouzo, Katarina."

In a single sip, the cold wine washes the dull sweetness from her mouth. And they begin to eat.

Jacqueline starts with the skewers of lamb, which are seasoned heavily with thyme. She feels her eyes well up. She closes them and continues to eat, the tears in the back of her throat combining with the meat.

There is her mother.

She opens her eyes.

There is Katarina.

There is one place, there is another.

There is the radiating sky, there is the moon.

"Good?" Katarina asks.

"Oh. Beyond that. Far, far beyond."

"I like the way you eat."

Jacqueline laughs and cuts into a pepper.

Easy, her mother says. Easy. You will make yourself sick.

Jacqueline obeys. She takes a breath, sits back, and has a sip of wine.

Katarina's question remains suspended.

"Where is your father?" Jacqueline asks.

"My father? He's in Skopje."

"Skopje?"

"Macedonia. We are from Macedonia."

"It's part of Greece?"

Katarina smiles. "It is two things. One is a part of Greece. One is a country. Mine is a country. You see? I don't know yours and you don't know mine."

"You're not Greek?"

"No."

"Macedonia," Jacqueline says.

"Yes. We are Macedonian. The summers I come to work."

"And Petros?"

"Greek. A friend of my father. For years a friend. Since I am a girl."

Jacqueline finishes the pepper, sits back, and drinks more of the wine.

"When do you go home?"

"September sometime. We will see with Anemomilos. And will see with the reservations here. I'm working here too sometimes when it is full."

Jacqueline nods. She is still drunk, but the speed of it, the wildness, is gone. She's calmer now. Slower. The rage has passed. She softens. She's becoming melancholic.

"September," she repeats. "And what month is it now, Katarina?"

The girl laughs and looks up from her plate, but when she sees Jacqueline looking at her she stops laughing. "You don't know what month is it?"

Jacqueline could pretend. Of course I do, she could say. Of course. It's just that here we lose track of time. Here on vacation. One cloudless day after another.

"Jacqueline?"

"No," she says. "I've lost track of time, Katarina. I've lost track completely."

"It is July. It is the very end. The very end of July."

Jacqueline nods.

She sees her cave.

She feels its damp stone against her hands.

She feels the cold wind blowing across the beach in Málaga. There are the carbon clouds barreling toward her, the rain coming again.

"You are a very strange woman, Jacqueline."

Jacqueline smiles and looks away. She can feel those eyes on her.

"I'm sorry, but what's happened? I don't understand. What is it?"

And again Jacqueline sees what she can do to her. Katarina the wondering and expectant child. The abandoned child, whose mother has forsaken her, mourning on her summer island.

You think you are so different? her mother says. You think you are so weary. So hardened. Look at yourself.

"What is it," Jacqueline repeats.

"Yes," Katarina says. "Please."

"Katarina," Jacqueline says as if she's speaking to a little girl.

Coward, her mother says. Coward. Weakling. Just like your father.

Already the girl has drawn back from the table to protect herself.

Coward, her mother says.

"Katarina," Jacqueline says again, this time not as the start of a sentence, but as if she's considering the beauty of the name. She pulls the bottle from the ice bucket, pours herself some wine, and empties the rest into the girl's glass.

"My father worked for the government. He was loyal and he was blind and he was stubborn. He was handsome and he was charming. He was very smart. That's what *he* was like." She blurts it all out fast.

He was an idiot, her mother says. Tell the goddamn truth if you're going to tell it, she says, drunk and slow.

"And he was an idiot," Jacqueline says. "A little boy."

Katarina picks up her wineglass and watches Jacqueline intently.

"He kept us there too long. There was a war. There *is* a war, for all I know. He kept us there too long and the soldiers came and they were the wrong soldiers. They weren't the ones he expected. The ones to protect us. We lived above the city and they came up the hill. Everyone had left. Our guards, our driver, our maid. They'd gone to hide or they'd gone to fight for the rebels, but they'd gone. So the soldiers came up the hill laughing, Katarina. They came and they cut through the fence like it was made of paper. They came up the hill and walked onto our lawn. They walked up the hill and through our fence and onto the lawn. A man and a group of boys. The boys carried rifles and machetes. They were dressed in T-shirts and shorts and rubber sandals. But the man was dressed like a soldier. He wore pants and boots and a red beret. A beard. There was a girl too. There was a girl. A tall girl with terrible eyes and rotten teeth.

"My sister was on the lawn. By then we never left the property. We were waiting for it all to pass, my father said. We were waiting for things to calm down, so that we could go back to our business, he said.

"So my sister was on the lawn walking around on the grass the way she liked to do. There was a cat. She'd started to feed an orange cat. A stray."

Jacqueline stops here.

Slow down, her mother says. You can breathe now and again, JaJa. Take your time.

Her mother was standing in a doorway. Jacqueline can't remember which. She was leaning against the frame with that wry expression on her face. She was holding a glass tumbler against the outside of her thigh, fingertips around the rim, nails painted pink.

Slow down when you tell a story, she says. Slow down.

Jacqueline nods. The sweating glass makes her mother's skin shine.

Jacqueline finishes her wine and goes on.

"My sister was out there on the lawn when they came up."

"What was your sister's name?" Katarina is very still.

"Saifa."

"I have three brothers," Katarina says.

"All those men."

"Please. I'm sorry to interrupt. Go on."

"The cat was gone by then," she says and looks down at the cold food. The enthusiasm she felt only a few minutes before is waning. For eating, for the story she has begun to tell.

"Please," Katarina says.

Go on, her mother says.

She draws a breath and continues.

"The cat was gone by then. When the boys cut through the fence and they came onto the grass, I was inside. They stood there looking around, smiling. No rush. Looking around like they were thinking of buying the house. The man with the beard, though. Did I tell you about him? I can't remember."

Katarina nods.

"He didn't smile. He passed the boys and crossed the yard and walked to my sister and took her by the throat with his left hand, the hand without the pistol, and marched her backward into the house. Right through the door where I was standing in the living room. He backed her up inside so that she was standing right next to me. Then he stepped back and looked at us.

"My sister was pregnant. Did I tell you that? She was enormous."

"No," Katarina says. "No." The girl has stopped moving. She has her hands on the table, one on top of the other.

"Yes. She was pregnant. Pregnant and no idea who the father was. Was. Is. I don't know. She always loved boys. She could never stay away from them. Not like me. I liked mine one at a time. And for a long time. And very few of them. Not that it did me any good. Maybe a little better. Maybe a lot better. Here I am with you, right? But Saifa, she liked to swim in them. From the time she was a girl. They made her drunk. Even when she was five years old. She was pregnant. That's the point now."

She pauses and for a moment she can't get a breath.

Katarina reaches across the table, and squeezes Jacqueline's forearm.

"Let's have more wine, Katarina. Please. Let's have another bottle."

"Yes. I will ask." And before Jacqueline can stop her, the

girl is up from the table, and with all the plates she can carry, is crossing the pool deck.

Shameful, her mother says. You could offer to help. Do something other than sitting here keeping yourself company. You and your self-pity. Get up and bring the rest of these plates.

Jacqueline begins to move, but it is too late. Katarina is returning with Petros, who follows with a tray under his arm, a bottle of wine in one hand, a bucket of ice in the other.

"You remind me of someone," Jacqueline says.

You are drunk, her mother says.

Katarina translates the sentence into Greek and Petros smiles, but says nothing.

Jacqueline doesn't know who he reminds her of.

There is a full bottle of wine and the table is cleared. The two women are alone again.

"Who does he remind you?"

Jacqueline shakes her head. "I can't remember," she says and raises her glass. "To Petros."

"Ouzo," Katarina says and gives her a weak smile.

The moon hangs above Nea Kameni, casting its light over the seething volcano.

"I will be very drunk soon."

"Me too."

"It's been a long, long time since I was drunk. It feels good, Katarina. It feels very good."

"You say my name very often, Jacqueline."

"Because it is a beautiful name, Katarina."

Katarina looks at her and smiles with such joy and sincerity that Jacqueline has to look away. She does not want to tell her story to this girl, this girl who can smile like that, who has the capacity for such brightness. But that's not right. She *does* want to tell her. She wants to tell the story more than ever now. But is telling it an act of violence? Is she using it to destroy the girl? Or is there some other reason? Why tell it otherwise? She has forgotten the reason for stories. For conversation. Perhaps she has never known the reason for them.

Perhaps, her father says. Perhaps.

She drinks more of the cold wine. The water looks so much like metal now that it stops being water. All the caldera is a sheet of finely cut metal.

You will end up like me, her mother says. If you continue to drink like this.

I don't have your tolerance.

No, her mother says. You are like your father that way.

"Is it true?" Jacqueline asks. "Is the volcano still alive?"

"Yes. You can go there and climb it and look inside and see."

Jacqueline nods.

"And there are places to swim. You can go and swim where the water is very warm and you can put some clay all over the skin. It is very good. We can go together if you like to."

"One day," Jacqueline says.

"Good."

"Are you afraid it will erupt again?"

Katarina shrugs her shoulders. "We all know it will happen one day. Or another earthquake. We are not a permanent place."

Her mother raises her eyes.

We are not a permanent place.

Jacqueline begins again, "'Where is your father?' the man said. Saifa lowered her head then. She just let it fall as if she'd gone to sleep all of a sudden. And me? I shrugged and didn't say anything. I didn't say anything until the man kicked Saifa in the belly and she fell over my father's reading chair and onto the floor. When he did that, I told him. I said, 'He's upstairs. Stop now. Stop now. Go get my father. Leave her,' as if I were in charge. The man looked at me and smiled for the first time. And then as he was smiling at me his boys came into the house. They wandered in with that same dazed look on their faces, like they were lost, or had woken up in some strange land. They came in and then behind them there was that tall girl and then the house felt very small with all those bodies spreading out in the living room. And then into other rooms. They were like oil flowing through the house, all of them so calm like they were half-asleep. And I kept worrying that one of them might not see Saifa, that one of them might step on her. That's how stupid I was. How far away I was from the world. That if they stepped on her it would be some kind of accident."

Jacqueline can smell the boys. They reek of sweat and cologne. Or perhaps those were the others. The boys on the side of the road. And for a moment she cannot remember which road that had been, or which boys. There were only the boys and the road and their cloying cologne. But then there is the rifle barrel and Bernard and his camera around her neck, and the strap cutting into her skin. So, she is able to sift through and organize it and return to where she was, so that she is ready to go on.

Jacqueline drinks more of her wine and then continues.

"I could feel the boys all around me. They were quiet. Like people in a museum. Wandering around, stopping and starting. But all the time I was facing the man. He was the pivot point. I knew that I should keep my eyes on him, that everything would begin there. Maybe I should have turned away. Maybe I should have gone to my sister. Knelt to take care of her. Knelt to the man. But I didn't. I stayed facing him, waiting for the next thing to happen. The two of us were still and all around was the slow motion of those boys. And then the girl. She brought my parents down the stairs and into the hall. It was a wide entryway with marble floors. And she brought my parents down. My mother said, 'You will burn in hell,' and I turned away from the man and he and I, we both looked over and there were my parents, standing side by side, and the tall girl with the yellow eyes standing behind them, holding two pistols out away from her body. The guns were at the ends of each of her straight arms. A barrel at the back of each of their heads and the girl was looking past them directly at the man with the beard. She was smiling at him. A tall girl with yellow eyes and a few rotting teeth smiling at a man with a beard in a red beret who was standing in our living room.

"'You'll burn in hell,' my mother said again, but all the anger had gone out of her voice. She said it now as a matter of fact. Quietly she said it. All this time my father was looking up at the ceiling. Not like he was praying, but as if he were trying to remember something he'd forgotten. "'Minister,' the man in the beard said then."

Jacqueline turns from the water and looks at Katarina. "My father was a finance minister. For the government."

The girl nods.

"Would you like me to go on? I can stop if you'd like. There's no reason to tell this story, Katarina."

Katarina looks at Jacqueline but doesn't speak, and for a moment Jacqueline thinks she will ask her to stop. And then she is disappointed. She isn't sure why she should be disappointed, why she wants to tell it, and while the two of them sit looking at each other with the wind blowing harder, Jacqueline drinks more of the wine and tries to work out why she wants to continue. What is the reason for telling this story to this girl? Earlier she'd wanted to do her harm, and that was one reason to tell it. But now she feels no desire to do her violence. She looks at her and she wants only to take her in her arms and kiss her hair and tell her that she is sorry for her loss, sorry her mother has died, that surely she knows what her mother was like, that even if she doesn't believe in God, or in heaven, or any of that garbage, her mother was there, in memory, in her, in the things Katarina says, in the way she treats people, in her conscience, in that voice that moves her through the world.

That is how she exists.

And in this way there is God. In this way there is no real death. In this way, Katarina, there is no real death.

Without consideration or preparation, she reaches out and wraps her hand around Katarina's forearm. Her fingers just below the elbow, she squeezes it gently. She wants to say everything to her, this girl who looks so young, holding her knees to her chest.

The wind is colder now and Jacqueline wants so much to take this girl into her arms, to draw her close, but she does not. She only offers her gentlest smile, and her warm hand on the girl's cool skin.

For an instant, she can feel Bernard's hands on her breasts, and his warm chest against her back, and his breath on her neck like a ghost.

"I don't have to finish the story," she says.

"No," Katarina responds and smiles back with a tenderness that strikes Jacqueline hard.

"No," she says again. "Please. I would like you to finish the story." And Jacqueline is relieved, because she wants to finish. She wants to tell it. And she wants to tell it to Katarina. Perhaps there is some reason for that.

Perhaps, her father says.

Perhaps, Jacqueline thinks, there is some reason that all the turns she's taken have brought her to this place. To this table, on this half-ruined island. To this hotel and its rectangle of green water. Here, sitting before this caldera, before this metal sea.

Perhaps, her father says.

God's will, her mother says.

Jacqueline draws her hand away carefully and pours them both more wine.

"I don't tell you the rest to hurt you," she says.

"No," Katarina says. "No. Of course."

Jacqueline can see that the girl doesn't understand. And now, listening to the words settling around her, she can't understand either. There is no logic to it. Yet it is important to say. And there are other things she wants to explain to the girl, but she isn't sure what they are or how to connect language to that want.

You're falling, her mother says. My heart. Don't do that. Just tell the girl. Tell us.

"The man in the beard said, 'Minister, look at me. Look at me.' And then my father lowered his eyes and looked. 'It is over now,' the man said. 'Taylor. You. Over. On this day. Understand me,' the man said. 'Understand me.' It wasn't a question, Katarina."

Katarina nods. "Taylor is your father?"

Jacqueline laughs. "Taylor was the president. My father's friend. My father's boss."

"And you liked him?"

"Yes, Katarina. I liked him. I liked him when he was in our home. I liked him when he brought me pretty boxes of Belgian chocolate. I liked him when he smiled at me. But I didn't know him. For a very long time, most of my life, I didn't know what he had done. And my father pretended not to know what he had done."

Katarina nods.

"But that is not this story. This story is the man with the beard who said, 'Do you see your daughters, Minister?'

"My father looked at me then for the first time since he'd come downstairs. There was nothing of him left. Nothing of him. He'd been draining out of himself for years. Or maybe it's the opposite of that. Maybe he'd been filling in. Slowly I'd been watching him become who he'd always been. The man my mother had come to know years earlier. All the charm. All that confidence. The lightness and humor. He looked at me and all I could see was fear. There was nothing else in his face. Not rage, not apology, nothing but fear."

Maybe love, Jacqueline thinks. But she cannot remember seeing love. She does not want to add that for the sake of the story. To appease the girl. She cannot remember love in his eyes, only fear, and so she will not include love.

"Only fear," she says. "That's all I saw and the man said, 'Do you see your daughters?' My father looked away from me then and scanned the room for my sister, but he couldn't find her because she was on the floor still. On the floor behind the reading chair, and when the man saw that she was out of my father's line of vision, he glanced at one of his boys, who jerked her up so that she was standing. 'Do you see your daughters?' the man repeated, and this time my father nodded. 'Speak,' the man said. 'Speak, Minister.'

"'Yes,' my father said, like a schoolboy before his teacher. 'Yes, I see my daughters.' He spoke with the weakest voice. A voice cracking in terror."

"You were not afraid?" Katarina asks.

"Yes," Jacqueline says. "I was afraid."

"So, not only him. All of you?" the girl asks, as if she wants to defend Jacqueline's father.

"No, not only him," Jacqueline agrees. "But somehow, somehow it was different."

"Are you sure he did not love you then? Maybe he loved you also. With everything else."

Jacqueline looks at the girl. "Maybe. Yes. Perhaps."

"You are angry," Katarina says. "I'm sorry."

The anger passes. "Perhaps you're right," Jacqueline says. "Perhaps it was love too."

Jacqueline's mother shakes her head.

And perhaps it was, Jacqueline thinks. Behind all the fear, and behind all that followed.

"'And do you see your wife, Minister?' the man said, and my father looked to his side and said yes, he saw his wife. 'Good,' the man said. 'Tell us their names. Introduce us, Minister, to your family.' And my father did it. 'This is my daughter Jacqueline. And this is my daughter Saifa. And this is my wife, Etweda.' He introduced us all in his cracking voice while we watched him. Then the man said, 'Good. Good. Now, Minister, now you can no longer pretend that we are not here.'

"'Please,' my father said then. And we waited to hear what he would say next, but he said nothing else. And then the man with the beard nodded at the girl, who stepped forward and pushed her pistols against my parents' skulls. I thought it would be then. I thought that was the signal to kill them, but I was wrong. Instead she pushed them forward and they disappeared into the kitchen, followed by a few of the floating boys. Then the man turned to me. 'Go stand with your sister,' he said, and I did. He didn't look at Saifa. He looked at me and then at Saifa's belly and then back at me. Then he smiled and said, 'So,' as if everything had become clear. 'Follow your parents,' he said, and we did.

"I took Saifa's hand. I led her into the kitchen. My parents were side by side on the floor. They were on their knees with their hands and feet bound behind their backs. When we walked in my father looked up at us and then he dropped his head and he began to cry.

"The kitchen was crowded with the boys. Some of them were sitting up on the counters and others were leaning against the oven. And the girl. She was leaning against the kitchen table."

Jacqueline finishes her glass of wine. She sees the tall girl and her terrible eyes and her rotted mouth. She sees the heavy table. Its polish. Its dark stain.

For a moment she can look through the glass door and across the lawn out to the storm clouds. Swollen slate balloons sagging with rain, and the palm trees bending and rustling loud in the wind.

And then again there is only the table.

"'Kneel,' the man said to me. And I knelt and let them tie my wrists. Let them tie my ankles. All without a fight. 'Kneel,' the man said, and I did.

"Katarina," Jacqueline says.

"Please," the girl says. She has released her legs and now she sits with both feet on the concrete. Her body is slumped in her chair, her arms crossed over her belly, fingers gripping her ribs. "Please," Katarina says. "Finish."

"There's no reason for it," Jacqueline says.

"Please."

"I was on my knees facing my parents with my back against some cabinets. I faced my parents, but it was only my mother's face I saw. My father hung his head, his chin against his chest, and he was weeping. My mother and I looked at each other. Her back was straight and she looked at me and I looked back. We were very much alike. Despite so many things, we were so much the same. She looked at me across the kitchen with Saifa standing at my side and my father kneeling at hers, and she looked at me so intently. We were separate, she and I. Always, the two of us, we were separate from them.

"Saifa hadn't been bound. She was the last of us to be free. I looked away from my mother and up at Saifa, who was standing very close to me. If I could have, I would have wrapped my arms around her legs. But I couldn't. So I just leaned to the side and pressed my cheek against her thigh. Her skin was very cold. And then the bearded man pushed her to the table."

Jacqueline draws the blanket higher around her shoulders, so that it covers the back of her neck. She is cold and very tired. She drinks more of the wine.

She wants to sleep.

She wants to climb into a soft bed in a black room and close her eyes.

Sleep and sleep and sleep.

Bernard, she thinks. Thinks his name. Thinks his body. His room. Their bed and the heavy air. Television strapped to the wall and a pyramid of oranges. She thinks of her cave and can feel her body inside it, her body entombed within all that rock.

There is the heavy kitchen table and the bearded man pushing Saifa toward it.

Katarina is watching her. Katarina waiting for the end.

"The man pushed her forward."

"Saifa?" Katarina asks.

It is the first time she's heard her sister's name spoken by someone else in what feels like years. The sound of it is devastating. She looks at Katarina, who tightens her lips, who seems to understand.

"My sister," Jacqueline says. "Saifa. Yes. He pushed her forward. He took her to the table and the boys tied her down. Boys. Just boys and they tied her down on her back, her arms and legs to the legs of the table. Maybe the man spoke. I don't know. But that's what they did. They tied her down on her back. Face up, you see? And there we all were. The kitchen full of us. Crowded with us. The ghost boys, the tall girl, the bearded man in his red beret, my sobbing father, me, my mother. And Saifa tied to the table.

"'Minister,' the man said. 'Minister, stand up.'

"My father tried to stand, but his legs must have been numb from kneeling and he fell. One of the boys yanked him to his feet by his wrists and held him there. 'Who do you love more?' the man asked. 'Wife or daughter?' He tried to answer. I looked up at him from the floor. He'd opened his mouth, but there was no noise. 'Wife or daughter?' the man asked again. This time he spoke louder. 'Minister,' he yelled now, but still my father said nothing. And then the man, he said, 'Okay, I choose,' and he raised his pistol and shot my mother just above her right ear. Just like that and she fell over onto her side. Then she was gone."

Katarina makes a noise and Jacqueline looks up. She looks up and reaches for the girl's hand.

"Katarina," Jacqueline says softly, trying to soothe her, pressing her hand. "It was better. It was better for her to die like that. To die *then*. Better for her."

Katarina draws her hand away. She finds a napkin, unfolds it, and holds it to her face. Then, after a long breath, she wipes her eyes and blows her nose.

"Finish," the girl says.

Jacqueline looks away.

She doesn't know.

She waits.

She has left Saifa there on her back, wrists and ankles bound to the legs of the table. She feels as if something has been suspended. She has left her sister while she waits on the floor, while her father cries and cries. Both of them impotent.

The only thing to do is to finish the story. You can't leave her there, she thinks.

You can't leave her there, her mother says, and Jacqueline goes on.

"Someone pulled me to my feet. One of the boys. Now I was standing on one side of the kitchen and my father was on the other. There was a boy behind each of us. All the rest of them, all the others were around the table.

"'Now we bet,' the man said. 'Now we bet,' he said, and the boys cheered. They cheered and the man smiled. 'Now we bet, Minister,' he said. He leaned in close to my father's ear and whispered something I couldn't hear. Then he stepped back and said, 'Well?' and my father, he just shook his head. 'Well?' the man said again louder.

"My father was silent. The man raised his hand and licked it wet enough to shine and then he slapped my father across the face. An open hand to the right cheek. Again and again, but still my father wouldn't speak, and after a while the man shrugged his shoulders like none of it mattered anyway. Then he looked at me. 'Watch,' he said and grinned. 'Watch.'"

Jacqueline can hear the wet cracking slaps. Can see the man's hideous pink tongue. Can see the side of her mother's shattered head resting on the tile.

The distance between recollection and experience is shortening. It is difficult to distinguish between memory and storytelling, between storytelling and experience, between this present life and the other. She is unsure whether there is a difference. She closes her eyes and tries to separate the filaments, tries to extricate one strand from another.

Her heart hammers against her breast. She is having trouble filling her lungs.

She keeps her eyes closed, but she goes on.

"'Saifa,' I said, 'Saifa,' but the man held up his hand. 'Don't speak. Watch,' he said. Then he turned his back to me and crossed the room. 'Bet,' he said, and the boys began to shout. 'Boy,' some of them said. 'Girl,' others said."

Suddenly Jacqueline is terrified that Katarina is gone, has left her. She opens her eyes and she's still there, still with her arms around herself, still slumped in the chair, but when she sees Jacqueline's face, she sits up straight and drags the chair forward. She raises her chin. As if to say, There is nothing you can tell me. There is nothing you can do.

Jacqueline looks at Katarina's eyes.

And she goes on.

"'Boy,' some of them said. 'Girl,' others said. One of the boys came to my father and pushed him forward so that he was closer to the table. And I stayed where I was.

"Saifa turned her head and looked at me. All this time she'd been looking above her, but now she turned her head and looked at me. Her cheek was pressed to the table and she looked at me. I looked back. Then she smiled. A gentle smile. Sad, as if she were worried about me. A smile of resignation. Lips pressed together, everything in the eyes. Then she turned and faced the wall.

"The boys were yelling louder now. You'd think I wouldn't have been able to stand. You'd think I would have fainted. But I stood there watching all of it. Doing nothing. Waiting. I didn't fight. I didn't scream. I didn't faint. I stood. That's what I did. I stood. I stood while my father cried. One of the boys was standing on a chair behind my father. On a chair, Katarina. So he could reach him. So he'd be tall enough. A little boy, and he had my father's head in the crook of his elbow, holding his head up, fingers on his eyelids, forcing him to watch. And then the tall girl came and stood at the end of the table. The boys were in a frenzy then. Screaming and screaming. Boy, boy, boy, girl, boy, girl, girl. Yelling and pounding the walls and slamming the chairs against the ground. Then my father began to scream, an awful high-pitched sound. Some of the boys began to mimic him then, trying to match their voices to his, trying to find his key. The noise was terrible. And me? I did nothing. I stood and I watched. I stood and I watched while the tall girl raised her machete and swung it down and split my sister's belly open."

Jacqueline hears the liquid sound of the cutting blade.

The sound is in her now.

In her throat.

In her stomach.

At the backs of her eyes.

She feels it there, pulsing. Some kind of living thing. It is breathing beneath her skin.

She looks at Katarina, who is leaning forward, elbows on the table, holding her head in her hands, eyes raised.

Jacqueline nods. "This is the story. One thing and then another thing and all these things in a row. One after another, you see? This is the story."

Katarina nods against her hands.

"There was a sound." Jacqueline shakes her head. "There was that sound and then when the girl withdrew the blade, the boys fell on her. On Saifa, who screamed in a voice I didn't recognize as hers and then she went silent and they fell on her and one of them reached inside and tore the baby out of her and held it up and screamed, girl, girl, girl, a girl. He cut the umbilical cord with his teeth and danced around the room with the baby above his head, singing his song, girl, girl, girl, until the man spoke and the boy brought it to my father. At first it was just a red mass of flesh. It could have been anything. But then I saw its legs and its arms and its little head bouncing on its limp neck and then it became what it was. A baby. A girl.

"'Closer,' the man said, and the boy pressed it to my father's closed mouth, smearing blood over his lips. 'What you have done to our country, we do to you,' the man said and looked at the boy and the boy raised the child and slammed it to the ground and the man raised his pistol and shot my sister three times. Then he looked at me. 'Watch,' he said, and pressed his gun to my father's skull and pulled the trigger. And that was the end. The man came to me and cut the rope from my wrists. He brought his mouth to my ear and he said, 'Tell it. You tell them what you've seen. You tell them what we are.'

"They left then. They left me in the kitchen alone with my family. And that was the end."

She stands from the table and walks to the edge of the terrace.

The dull point of the black volcano has pierced the moon.

The soft wind rises from the caldera and Jacqueline draws it into herself.

She can breathe.

Her heart has stopped its hammering.

Still there is the sound.

"Jacqueline," Katarina says.

The girl is at her side now. The two of them stand together looking out over the cliff, across the silver water.

"Jacqueline," Katarina says again, and now the girl reaches for her. She reaches out with her arms and Jacqueline allows it. She allows herself to be drawn into the girl's body and soon she brings her own arms around the girl.

They hold each other there on the edge of the terrace, at the edge of the cliff, in the disappearing moonlight. The two of them in the wind and Jacqueline closes her eyes.

Her heart is slow. Her mind is quiet.

She raises her right hand and cups the back of Katarina's head.

"Shh," Jacqueline says to the girl. "Shh."

JACQUELINE WILL WALK home before dawn.

She will walk through the silent marble streets, past the feral dogs, past the locked church and its empty square.

She will take the long way and go out to the fort and stand above the village.

She will look back at the lights of Imerovigli and Fira and beyond to the lightening sky.

She will try to make out the silhouette of the rose church.

She will guess which bead of glass is Petros, which light is Anemomilos, which shadow is Katarina.

She will turn and face the open sea and look across the water to the shifting ghost islands purple in the distance and she will try to decide if she should stay here or continue on to somewhere else.

She will pass the bus station and turn down the asphalt road and then onto the dirt and she will walk until she finds her hotel.

Inside, in the faint light, she will remove her clothes and slip into bed.

She will feel Saifa's feet in her hands.

She will see her father's gentle eyes.

She will see the bearded man and the tall girl and her moldering teeth.

She will hear the sound, the splitting blade.

She will hear the rattle of ice against glass.

She will feel that warm palm pressing against her chest.

She will fall heavy into sleep.

Just like the dead, her mother will say in the late afternoon when Jacqueline first opens her eyes.

You've slept just like the dead, JaJa.

JaJa, my love, my heart.

Acknowledgments

I am grateful to the following people and institutions:

To Jonathan Stack, James Brabazon, and Tim Hetherington for their extraordinary film, *Liberia: An Uncivil War*, as well as to Gini Reticker, Abigail E. Disney and Kirsten Johnson for their film, *Pray the Devil Back to Hell*. And again to Tim Hetherington for his book *Long Story Bit by Bit: Liberia Retold*, and to Helene Cooper for her memoir, *The House at Sugar Beach*.

To Lan Samantha Chang, Connie Brothers, and the Iowa Writers' Workshop for their support—emotional, financial, literary—and for providing the most stable home I've known in years.

To the Truman Capote Literary Trust for the means to write without any other obligation. I cannot imagine a greater gift.

To Eric Simonoff, who has been there from the start—wise and unwavering.

To Jordan Pavlin, who fought so hard for this novel, has so much faith in me, and manages to be so many good and disparate things at once.

To Kimberly Burns, advisor, advocate, and indefatigable friend.

To Madhuri Vijay, who read a thousand times, and always came riding around the corner.

To Dorothy Royle, for listening to every word—may this book be a talisman.

To Allan Gurganus, whose teaching was a revelation.

To Merritt Tierce, for all of it.

To my generous friends and readers, Ayana Mathis, Jon Brockett, Jason Martin, Pascale Brevet, Grant Rosenberg, and John McNulty, for their patience, counsel, encouragement, and kindness.

To Anthony Marra, partner in writing what we do not know.

ACKNOWLEDGMENTS

To Sarah Hedrick and Jan Weissmiller, for Iconoclast and Prairie Lights, respectively—homes away from homes.

I wrote this novel while constantly moving from place to place, and everywhere I went people welcomed me. In Los Angeles, particular thanks to my old friends James and Nina Tooley, who keep opening their door. In Estonia, thank you to Marika Blossfeldt and the Polli Talu Arts Center. In Paia, thanks to Karen Bouris and Rob Hilbun. In New York, to Mark and Jill Eshman, who very literally provided shelter from the storm. In Paris, to Andy Scisco and Ina Stolen for their apartment and that famous kitchen. In Ketchum, thanks (twice) to Barbara Boswell, to Ray and Wendy Cairncross, Margo Peck, and Lyman and Debra Drake.

Thank you also to Pilar Guzman, Michael Reynolds, Peter Orner, Nikki Terry, Erik Leidecker, Gretchen Wagner, Steven and Elena Younger, Bob and Barbara Goodkind, Ethan Canin, Joe Blair, Caroline Bleeke, Peter Mendelsund, Lena Little, Paul Bogaards, Roland Philipps, Eleanor Birne, Cathryn Summerhayes, Laura Bonner, Claudia Ballard, and Kate Hutchison.

Finally, to my parents, without whom none of this. With all the love I have.